SHERLOCK HOLMES
AND
THE REAL THING

ALSO BY
NICHOLAS MEYER

FICTION

Sherlock Holmes and The Telegram from Hell

From the memoirs of John H. Watson

The Seven-Per-Cent Solution

The West End Horror

The Canary Trainer

The Adventure of the Peculiar Protocols

The Return of the Pharaoh

Target Practice

Black Orchid (with Barry Jay Kaplan)

Confessions of a Homing Pigeon

NONFICTION

The Love Story Story

The View From the Bridge — Memories of Star Trek and a Life in Hollywood

SHERLOCK HOLMES
AND
THE REAL THING

A CASE HISTORY RECORDED BY JOHN H. WATSON, M.D.

EDITED BY
NICHOLAS MEYER

THE MYSTERIOUS PRESS
NEW YORK

SHERLOCK HOLMES AND THE REAL THING

Mysterious Press
An Imprint of Penzler Publishers
58 Warren Street
New York, N.Y. 10007

Copyright © 2025 by Nicholas Meyer

First edition

Interior design by Maria Fernandez

All rights reserved. No part of this book may be reproduced in whole or in part without written permission from the publisher, except by reviewers who may quote brief excerpts in connection with a review in a newspaper, magazine, or electronic publication; nor may any part of this book be reproduced, stored in a retrieval system, or transmitted in any form or by any means electronic, mechanical, photocopying, recording, or other, or used to train generative artificial intelligence (AI) technologies, without written permission from the publisher.

Library of Congress Control Number: 2024950103

ISBN: 978-1-61316-656-7
eBook ISBN: 978-1-61316-657-4

10 9 8 7 6 5 4 3 2 1

Printed in the United States of America

*For my sisters
Constance, Juliette, and Deborah Abigail
and my daughters
Dylan, Madeline, and Roxanne Drew
and my nieces
Natasha, Tatiana, Jennifer, and Amanda*

When the flush of a new-born sun fell first on Eden's green and gold,
Our father Adam sat under the Tree and scratched with a stick in the mould;
And the first rude sketch that the world had seen was joy to his mighty heart,
Till the Devil whispered behind the leaves: "It's pretty, but is it Art?"

—Rudyard Kipling

ABOUT THIS BOOK

I now have a website. The primary purpose is hawking my brand, selling merch (my books), touting my in-person appearances, etc.

There's also a place where "the public" (that would be you) could "contact me" (that would be—you get the idea).

Most of these communications are swell. ("I really like your books.") Some are questions. ("Why did Kirk's son where a sweater?" Spelling is sometimes interesting.)

Some are requests. ("Would you sign my Company Business poster?" "Would you be on my podcast?", etc.)

Some are not so nice. ("You stink." "I hated Wrath of Khan!" "Election was stolen!", etc.)

But a year or so back, I read this one (typos included):

> Dear Mr. Meyer, I know from *West End Horror* you are always getting missing Dr. Watson manuscripts to edit

so here's one more. This is not BS! I live in Boca Raton and our library was unloading bunches of books we're not allowed to keep on our shelves anymore, so anyone could take some. This folder with typed pages was in the kids' section which is how come they had to throw it away. I took it home and read it. It kinda freaked me out so I get why it's not allowed in the kids section but I showed it to my dad and asked what to do with it. He said maybe get in touch with you which I saw how on your website. If you'd like to take a look we could figure out how to get thefolder to you. I bet you probably don't give out your address. It's too big for me to scan (I have finals coming up), but after that maybe get the pages photocopied if you tellme where to send them? I'm scanning a few pages and pasting them so you get the idea.

I can't tell if they're real, but maybe you do?

Very truly yours, Michael Abernathy Jr. [14]

As the writer correctly understands, over the years I've received or been offered a lot of these things in one form or another. Most of them *are*, as he says, BS.

For that reason, and because I have other obligations, I didn't intend to bother with the four scanned pages that were included in the website letter.

But the pages were right there on the screen below the letter, so I thought, *What the heck.*

To make a long story short, I didn't (and still don't) know if what I read is authentic. It's not like the pages were handwritten

ABOUT THIS BOOK

or anything so convenient that might offer clues. And there wasn't even any physical paper to inspect. It's just images on my screen.

On the other hand, I *did* want to know what happened next, which is why I answered young Abernathy's online submission and waited for his finals to be over (he says he passed), and offered to pay for photocopying the rest of the pages and send me the originals but at that point Abernathy Sr. got cagey and said we could talk about that later.

Well, it *is* later and the Abernathys have gone silent, but two weeks after I made my offer, I did get the rest of the photocopied pages (not the originals), in a package addressed to me care of my agent, with no return address, only a Baton Rouge postmark and "fragile" scrawled in blue magic marker. I can't say why but I've the hunch Abernathy Sr. wasn't informed about this. As for the contents, I can't vouch for much as I don't even have the actual pages to study, but I did have the font looked at (there are people who are into this stuff) and am told it comes from a Blickensderfer No. 5 portable typewriter, circa 1896, so at least that part is in the right ballpark.

It's hard for me to read anything without automatically reaching for a Uniball, so I performed minor editing chores along the way. The original orthography is British rather than American but anyone can do that. And there's stuff I know can't be right (e.g.: when Watson says he and Holmes saw Houdini perform in London would seem to be off *by years*), but that could be a memory lapse on W's part. A few times I added what I hope are helpful footnotes but you can always skip them.

I have no idea if what I've cleaned up is real but it kept me reading and I learned a lot of miscellaneous stuff I previously knew

ABOUT THIS BOOK

nothing about. To me it reads like Watson but that doesn't mean anything these days. Maybe this is all ChatGPT. But we all want to believe.

What do you think?

Nicholas Meyer
Los Angeles, 2024

I

THE MIRACLE

Sherlock Holmes was bored. For the ruck of humanity, boredom is at worst an irritant or annoyance, but for the detective it constituted anathema. It required no great powers of observation on my part to diagnose his condition, though Holmes had often twitted me regarding my deficiencies ("you observe but you do not *see*," he liked to say), for the symptoms in this instance were plain enough.

His researches into the mating habits of red ants lay scattered about the rug. Treatises on the Battle of Lepanto were likewise abandoned, while monographs on the dietary requirements of the Costa Rican sloth gathered dust below the deal table containing his malodorous chemical experiments, and these had not been touched in weeks. For this I was grateful, as the frigid weather made it impossible to open a window and the accumulation of pipe smoke as our confinement lengthened was bad enough. The haze in our sitting room was almost as impenetrable as a London fog.

But, as if to prove clues unnecessary, Holmes proclaimed his malaise in no uncertain terms. "I am stagnating, Watson! My brain requires activity the way a locomotive demands coal. Without both, everything grinds to a halt!"

We were in fact running short of coal by this time. Should resupply not arrive by the week's end, our situation would deteriorate from uncomfortable to perilous. For the better part of a month we had been shut-ins, the result of a succession of late winter storms that pelted London with heaps and drifts of snow, clogging the great city's arteries and bringing the nexus of civilization to a standstill. Each time the sweepers attempted to make headway, another silent white tempest would arrive, undoing their progress. Service on the Underground was intermittent and deliveries, whether by post or from the greengrocer, ceased altogether; even the papers no longer arrived. This last was yet another straw laden on the camel's back, for Holmes was devoted to the agony notices, forever poring over each dolorous message in hopes of spotting something outré into which he could sink his teeth. His crestfallen expression this morning told me he had come up empty.

"It's enough to make me cancel my subscription," said he, contemptuously tossing aside a week-old number of *The Globe*. "What sort of newspaper is it that cannot muster content for its own agony column? A shoddy enterprise at best," he fumed.

The crime famine was driving him to distraction. On several previous occasions indeed ("the years of plenty," in his words), cases with what he called "features of interest" had trooped to our door, allowing Holmes to demonstrate his unique gifts to their fullest extent. Often momentous outcomes proved to be at stake, but in this fierce winter the pickings were few and scarce. Holmes was prepared to settle for some seemingly inconsequential difficulties, those not played out in the headlines or on the international stage, but which nonetheless gave him the opportunity and motive to put his brain in gear. It is one such case I now relate. It began innocuously enough with a seemingly trivial matter, but proved more sinister than either the detective or myself could have imagined. At one end was nothing more remarkable than overdue rent; at the other lay four corpses.

And, as it happened, it was a case that changed my life.

Prior to the onset of inclement weather, Holmes had solved the case of the purloined otter (an otter for which the world is not yet prepared) by cleverly noting the trail of koi heads leading from the Serpentine. A substantial reward was offered by the nobleman in question as well as an impressive medal issued by a foreign power, both of which the detective declined with lofty condescension.* ("My fees are on a fixed scale and I require no additional remuneration.") And nothing in the way of interest had appeared either in the post or on our doorstep since then.

"Trifles, Watson," he would say, heaving a theatrical sigh. "Nothing worth my attention. I ask you, what is the world coming to?"

"It may be the world is improving," I ventured to suggest, "at any rate, when the weather clears, perhaps—"

---

* The nobleman appears to have been Graf Otto Helmuth von Holstein-Thyssen of Croatia, a fish lover with a vast estate and animal preserve in Kent. The Croatian medal in question features an image of St. Donatus of Zadar.

"Improving? Perish the thought! And rob me of my livelihood? It's very good of you, my dear fellow," he went on, packing his blackened cherrywood with shag, "trying to raise my spirits, but I'm afraid it won't do. I am in need of a miracle and miracles, it appears, are out of season. Without divine intervention, I shall subside into one of my spells of indolence and lassitude where I am quickly beyond redemption."

I dreaded to hear these last words, for when the fit was on him, the detective had been known to drowse for days on end. This remedy thankfully seemed not to occur to him. Abruptly disdaining his pipe, now indifferent to the consolations of tobacco in addition to all else, he took out his prized Stradivarius and began tuning it. At this my spirits rose. Despite his disclaimers, my friend was an excellent violinist. I anticipated a concert (I was partial to his variations on "Poor Little Buttercup"), but instead he set the instrument across his knee and began idly sawing away at the strings, producing some of those queer sounds he favored when the standard repertoire failed to engage his interest or challenge his abilities.

The violin's unsettling moans did nothing to improve my humour but I judged them preferable to some of Holmes's previous alternatives to ennui. In similar straits, Holmes had amused himself by using my old service revolver for indoor target practice, once going so far as to spell out the initials *V. R.* above the hearth in bullet pocks before an outraged Mrs. Hudson put a stop to it. Neighbors were complaining, she informed him, warning that if he persisted, constables would shortly be breaking down the door.

At least he no longer had recourse to an earlier solution, a seven-per-cent mixture of cocaine and distilled water, taken intra syringe. As his friend as well as medical man, I had strenuously protested this practice from the time I first learned of it. One day perhaps I shall detail the sensational circumstances under which he finally rid himself of this loathsome habit.*

"For all we know war with the Boers has broken out," the detective mused, still producing unfortunate wails on his instrument. The fact that Holmes seldom took any interest in politics only served to indicate to what extremities our situation had reduced him.

It was with relief as well as astonishment that I beheld a hansom drawn by a blanketed horse, whose quivering nostrils exhaled steam, struggling to a stop amid waist-high snowdrifts below our window.

"I say, Holmes, I think we are about to receive a visitor."

"Nonsense." The infernal squeaks continued.

"A woman."

Behind me, the wails persisted.

"Veiled," I threw in.

"Really?" He stopped playing. "I suspect you are embellishing already."

"Well, enveloped in a muffler," I conceded. I had added a veil in hopes of diverting him.

---

* A full account of Holmes's cocaine cure is to be found in *The Seven-Per-Cent Solution*.

The figure disappeared from view. The cab remained where it was. The driver, his face swaddled in a thick yellow scarf, huddled miserably under another blanket. Shortly thereafter, we heard the bell at 221.

"To be out on such a morning as this," I went on, "I suspect her errand is an urgent one. That she has taken a cab suggests a certain affluence."

"Unless someone else has paid for the cab," was Holmes's only comment.

In the event, both my assertions proved correct. Presently, Mrs. Hudson knocked briskly at our door and handed the detective a salver upon which reposed a white visiting card.

"Lady Glendenning is below," she informed us, unable to resist casting a disapproving eye at our chaotic, smoke-filled rooms. "She says the matter is of utmost importance."

Holmes examined the card, holding it up to the light, waving it back and forth under his nose, going so far as to sniff the engraved font.

"Bembo twelve point two," he observed.

"Holmes, for heaven's sake."

"Very well, Mrs. Hudson, you may ask the young woman to come up."

"How do you know she's young?" I asked when the door was closed.

"The card is scented," he replied, carefully setting aside his violin. "That is lately the fashion. It is a long shot but in moments we shall learn if I've hit the mark."

"The only Glendenning I've ever heard of is Glendenning Properties," I said.

"Yes, one sees those estate placards throughout the city."

In anticipation of the new arrival, we rose to our feet.

"I wonder if this will prove miraculous," Holmes murmured as we could now make out the tread on the stair.

In fact the visitor who presented herself was neither young nor old, but a lady of middle years, comely and well-dressed, but not conspicuously so, with a full figure and eyes of a remarkable sapphire blue. On her left cheek was an attractive mole of the sort fashionable women in an earlier era supplied with cosmetics. Her hat, coat, and muffler she had deposited in the entryway, revealing her most striking feature, a head of almost white-blonde hair of the type sometimes called platinum. She looked from one to the other of us uncertainly.

"Mr. Holmes?" She was slightly out of breath from the seventeen steps.

"I am Sherlock Holmes," said my friend. "This is my associate, Dr. Watson, before whom you may speak as freely as myself."

"Yes, I thought as much." Lady Glendenning offered a tentative smile. "If I may say so, you look rather like your pictures."

"Too kind," said the detective producing a smile of his own. "Allow me to offer my condolences on your recent loss."

Our visitor's eyes blinked in confusion. "My loss? How did you—Oh!"

With mild surprise, Lady Glendenning followed the detective's gaze to the black crepe on her left sleeve.

"Ah, yes, my mourning band. The act of sliding it on each day has become so reflexive I keep forgetting what it proclaims to others. Lord Glendenning died almost six months ago."

"I recall reading of his death," said Holmes in a soothing tone. "Won't you tell us what has happened? Would you like some tea?"

"Thank you, no." In the silence that followed, we waited expectantly. Lady Glendenning stood irresolutely on the hearthrug, taking in our furnishings, whose eccentricity struck me with renewed force as seen through the eyes of a stranger. Without turning to see, I knew the detective to be taking a detailed inventory of our visitor.

"Pray sit, Lady Glendenning. A journey in this weather has certainly tired you."

"It has." The woman snapped out of her trance and settled into the high-backed horsehair customarily reserved for visitors as we drew up our chairs. "Rupert Milestone has disappeared." The lady made this announcement as though she anticipated the name would produce an effect, but seeing it made none, she went on. "Rupert Milestone, the artist. Surely you are familiar with his work?"

Holmes shook his head. "Though my family tree does boast a distinguished painter* and while I possess some incidental knowledge, I must confess that music rather than art is more my line. Mr. Milestone is—"

---

* Holmes claims descent from the sister of the French artist, Émile-Jean-Horace Vernet.

"Mr. Milestone is a well-regarded portraitist. His rendering of Lady Windermere is very well known, if a trifle risqué," she added, lowering her voice. "He is also my tenant."

"Your tenant?"

"Oh, I see. I'm so muddled." Again glancing uncertainly at her surroundings, Lady Glendenning gave the impression she wished she were elsewhere. "Permit me to explain. Lord Glendenning owns, or rather owned, a good deal of property in town."

"One sees the Glendenning name on leaseholds everywhere," I interposed.

"That is so, doctor," she inclined her head in my direction. "But though we are well-off, my late husband was intermittently disposed to fits of what he termed, 'economy.' Penny-pinching, some might call it." She shook her head with a trace of embarrassment. "He involved himself in all aspects of his business and since his demise, it has fallen to me to manage his affairs, rather a complicated undertaking as I am—or should say, was—inexperienced in these matters. Many of Basil's—Lord Glendenning's—properties are let or leased all over the city. We have clerks and bookkeepers, to be sure, but for more time than I would wish, a great many tiresome details are now my responsibility, as they were his. It's all I can do to keep track of lease renewals, leaky taps, cracked drainpipes, and window sashes that require—"

The detective laid a soothing hand on her arm. "What has happened to Mr. Milestone? Pray be as precise as possible."

"That's just it," said our visitor, her voice rising slightly. "I don't know what has happened to him. What I *do* know is that he's not paid his rent."

Holmes tried to suppress any trace of disappointment. Lady Glendenning was not the sort of miracle he had in mind, but he determined to do the best he could with the hand fate had dealt. "Is that customary on Mr. Milestone's part?"

Her next sentence proved more encouraging. "By no means! These last four years the man has been punctuality itself. Tenants frequently fall behind. It's an occupational hazard for landlords, but Mr. Milestone is reliable as clockwork. Four years ago he let a large atelier of ours in Notting Hill, 'round the corner from the Underground. The studio was purpose-built by Burne-Jones and features a skylight and small but sufficient adjacent living quarters. I never heard his lordship complain of or ever known Mr. Milestone to be in arrears, but it's been three months and despite leaving repeated messages, I've not heard a word."

"Since before Christmas then?"

She nodded. "Nor seen any of the rent," she added with a sniff. "I dropped by the studio two days ago and, hearing no answer, let myself in."

"Let yourself in?" Holmes's question prompted a blush.

"With so many properties, I find myself a veritable turnkey. I am obliged to carry a weighty valise of latch and passkeys that open doors all over the city, though I seldom have occasion to use them. Truthfully, it's more a ball and chain, but in this instance I felt I must get to the bottom of things," she added as if to justify her action.

"And?" Holmes had begun to hope.

"There was no sign, Mr. Holmes. The place was empty and dusty. And the unopened post was piled up inside the door."

"Dusty?"

"It was evident no one had been within for some time. Perhaps weeks. I've no way of telling, but since the rent has not been paid in over three months—"

"Mr. Milestone employs no housekeeper or charwoman?"

"If he did I saw no evidence of her presence." Lady Glendenning pushed aside a stray lock of white-gold hair. "I once offered him a recommendation but he only expressed irritation with the idea. 'She will get underfoot and disturb my concentration,' he said, or some such words to that effect. Oh, I know, Mr. Holmes, I just know, something is amiss." Lady Glendenning was unable to suppress wringing her hands, still clad in the dark kid gloves she had failed to shed downstairs.

"Do take some tea," I said, pouring from the pot. "It will do you good."

She favored me with a look of relief and began tugging off the gloves, the right hand appearing to present some difficulty. "Thank you, doctor, I think perhaps you are right. I confess I am at my wits' end."

When the glove was removed, we saw the cause of the difficulty: a ruby the size of a quail's egg in a gold setting on the lady's third finger.

"Try to remember the smallest detail, even if you think it unimportant, Lady Glendenning," said Holmes. "Apart from the dust, did you observe anything unusual?"

Lady Glendenning's brows contracted in thought. "Not that I recall."

Holmes closed his eyes and pressed the tips of his fingers together, trying his best, I knew, not to appear pleased. "No clothing scattered about? Nothing conspicuously missing or out of place? Any new or unfamiliar item you had not seen before?"

"I don't think so." She absently rubbed the ring against her lips.

"What about his work?"

"The pictures? There were plenty in evidence. On the few occasions I was inside, the studio was always full of stacked canvases and smelled pleasantly of oil paint and linseed. On my last visit, a drop cloth covered his easel but I didn't think to remove it."

"And when you found Mr. Milestone's abode in the state you describe, what did you do next?"

"I went to the police, Mr. Holmes. Perhaps you will think I reacted disproportionately—"

"Not at all. Yours seems a perfectly natural response, given what you have told us. Pray continue and try to remember in detail what happened. Trifles in such matters may prove crucial."

She nodded. "I told the police what I have told you. But they didn't seem much interested. An Inspector Gregson suggested Mr. Milestone might be on holiday."

"Ah, yes," murmured Holmes, "that sounds like Gregson."

"Or Lestrade," I felt bound to add.

Our sarcasm was lost on Lady Glendenning.

"When I assured the inspector this was most unlikely, he suggested I file a missing person's report and so I did. But oh," her voice rose again, "I just know something untoward has happened. I tell you I can feel it in my bones and I am seldom wrong about these things! When I returned to the police and renewed my concerns, the inspector suggested that perhaps I ought to contact you. And here I am." Having concluded her recital, she drew a deep breath as if a heavy weight had been lifted and sipped some tea.

Holmes took his time relighting his pipe, using tongs to pick up a glowing coal from the grate and drawing contentedly on the pleasing aroma. "Watson," said he at length, "do you think the Circle Line is running today and might carry us as far as Notting Hill Gate?" He turned to our new client. "If the train is in operation, would you be willing for Dr. Watson and myself to examine your tenant's premises? Say in an hour's time? In your presence, to be sure."

"So soon?" Lady Glendenning, I could see, was surprised by the detective's timetable.

"If something untoward has in fact occurred," Holmes explained, "the longer our investigation is delayed, the colder the trail is likely to become. And if, as you tell it, Mr. Milestone has not been heard from in months, the trail seems already rather chilly."

"Oh, I see," the lady responded with a sigh of relief. "Oh, thank you, Mr. Holmes. I shall be at number 7 Turncoat Lane* in one hour. Thank you both," she added, setting down her cup and rising to her feet.

"Will you be all right outdoors?" I asked, holding the door for her and gesturing to the snow flurries outside our window.

"Now that I am a landlady, I find myself obliged to travel in all weathers," she answered with an air of resignation, "and my driver is waiting. The Circle Line is running—or it was this morning. I

---

* Today Campden Hill Road.

shall expect you both in an hour. Thank you again, gentlemen. I cannot begin to express my gratitude."

"Well, Watson, what do you make of it?" Holmes asked after Lady Glendenning's descending footfalls had died away. He was swirling the teapot to ascertain how much remained within.

"Most peculiar."

"Or most ordinary. Nine times out of ten what seems inexplicable turns out to have the most disappointing explanation. You will recall how stunning it was when we saw the great Houdini walk through a solid brick wall last March at the Hippodrome."

"I still cannot make heads or tails of that. The bricks were laid before our eyes, perpendicular to the stalls, such that we could see on either side of what soon became a six-foot-high wall. The bricks were laid directly over a large red carpet to preclude the use of trap doors. Hammer and nails were provided and the audience was invited to come on stage and pound in as many as they pleased. I believe I hammered one or two nails into that carpet myself."

"You did. I remember the evening quite well. When the wall was complete, two Chinese screens were placed on either side. Houdini disappeared behind one screen and within less than a second reappeared behind the other on the opposite side of the wall. The audience went wild."

"But how on earth . . . ?"

"Think, Watson. Why the two screens? There can only be one answer: to prevent us seeing the moment when the magician actually passed through a brick wall."

"Then—"

Holmes chuckled. "Of course there was a trap door."

"But the rug—!" I protested, prompting an additional laugh.

"Houdini had no need to go *through* the rug. When the magician disappeared behind the first Chinese screen, his confederate beneath the stage opened the trap door directly under the wall, creating a *sag* in the rug. The rug covering the trap door had just enough slack over the opening to allow him to roll *under* the wall and straighten himself up on the other side an instant before emerging from the screen on the other. As he did so, the confederate closed the trap door and the floor appeared as solid and undisturbed as ever."

"You know this? Someone revealed the secret?"

He shrugged. "I deduced it. "My dear Watson, no one can walk through a brick wall. Eliminate the impossible—"

"And whatever remains—" I had heard this maxim often enough to repeat it in my dreams. "Holmes what are you doing?"

The detective was perched on our stepladder, awkwardly lowering three heavy volumes.

"Behold! Debrett's, Burke's, and the Almanach de Gotha. I think it's as well to learn what we can of Lord Glendenning and his lady. Do dress warmly, old man," he added, thumbing through Debrett's. "It won't do for either of us to catch colds."

With an exclamation of satisfaction, the tome was abandoned like so many others and he began throwing on layers of clothing when a thought caused him to stop in midmotion. "I say, Watson, a forced march to Edgware Road in all this"—his hand took in the world outside our window—"may be too much for your leg. I'm quite capable of going it alone."

"Nonsense," I retorted. "After being cooped up all this time, the air will do me good."

Though the flurries ceased, the sky remained overcast and the arctic air cut like a knife. Mercifully, there was no wind. In truth, a forced march through dirty snow drifts to Edgware Road was precisely what ensued and my penang lawyer proved essential to my ability to carry on. By the time we reached the Edgware Road station, our trouser legs were soaked and I was spent.

Holmes did not enjoy the Underground and seldom made use of it, preferring to be where he could see the world, but I knew the prospect of being tardy unsettled him. With me, he might be late or sometimes disappear altogether for days on end if an investigation demanded it, but his business acumen told him that clients do not expect to be kept waiting—especially a new, well-to-do client.

The station, like the road above it, was almost deserted when we descended into its sooty warmth, but there was no train to be seen.

More to distract himself, I suspect, than enlighten me, the detective relayed what he had found in Debrett's: "The Glendenning line goes back to the twelfth century and Dumfriesshire. Their coat of arms, let me see,"—he screwed up his features in an attempt to recall arcane terminology—"a sable quartered argent and rampant with gules, no that can't be right—" he stamped his feet impatiently, eyeing the cavernous dark maw at the end of the platform. In the interim, more prospective riders filled the platform. Holmes consulted his watch.

"A watched kettle," I reminded the detective. "Do go on, Holmes."

He complied with a sullen grace. "The late Lord Glendenning's first wife died over thirty years ago. There is a daughter, who seems to live in Australia, if she is alive. The late widower remarried our client some five years ago. Ah, here at last!"

He broke off his summary as the train roared in, crammed with riders. It was all we could do to force our way aboard with the Edgware Road passengers crowding behind us. The atmosphere inside the carriage was stifling, all those overcoats and mufflers stuffed together like—

"Our client lacks any trace of blue blood," the detective, speaking into my ear, resumed where he had left off. "She is one Vera Pertwee from Islington."

"Islington?"

"Did you not hear the lady's distinctive East London accent? And if Debrett's is describing the same Lady Glendenning, she is twenty-three years younger than her late husband."

"Such liaisons are not unheard of," I felt bound to point out. "But how might their paths have crossed? Vera Pertwee as was from Islington is not likely to have frequented Pall Mall or the Ritz. And I can't see the lady as a guest at Boodles."

"I don't see that presents any great difficulty. Lord Glendenning owned and administered property all over town. It is not beyond the realm of possibility that Miss Pertwee was herself a tenant. Perhaps hers was one of the leaky pipes she felt bound to call to her landlord's attention."

Sometimes it was hard to know if the detective was joking.

"If she set her cap for him—" I began.

"She was indeed aiming high," he agreed. "But if battles have been lost for want of a horseshoe nail, is it not possible that something as trivial as a squeaking door hinge might also alter the course of history? However they met," he continued, "the marriage seems to have produced no offspring."

"Would you call that 'suggestive'?"

"I might."

"So Lady Glendenning is now a wealthy widow," began my summation. "We saw that ruby—"

"Not a ruby, Watson, but a carbuncle, sometimes called a garnet, traditionally red in colour. Nonetheless your point is taken. Lady Glendenning may now command as many hansoms as she pleases. A whole fleet, if she chooses. And have the drivers wait upon her all day, miserable as they may be, huddled in their blankets."

"To say nothing of the horse," I began when he interrupted me with a cry.

"Ah, here is Notting Hill Gate at last!"

2

PORTRAIT OF THE ARTIST

"You had no trouble finding it?" inquired Lady Glendenning. "I know it's a bit of a walk from the Underground in this weather."

The h in *had* was conspicuously shortchanged. Now that Holmes had drawn my attention to it, I had no trouble recognizing the faint traces of cockney and Lady Glendenning's efforts to suppress them.

"Do come in, gentlemen."

The vast, unheated room in which we found ourselves conformed to our client's description. Perhaps seventy feet in length and roughly forty in width, it boasted a high ceiling entirely comprised of a skylight, whose cast-iron struts supported enormous glass panels. Under ordinary circumstances, I judged it would provide a painter with ample daylight and likely some warmth as well, but at present the glass was entirely blanketed with snow, rendering the chilly place in which we stood dark, until Lady Glendenning lit the gas. It occurred to me that if the snow resumed, it was possible the skylight might give way under its weight.

"It was purpose built to withstand the weather," Lady Glendenning said, following my look. "By Burne-Jones," she reminded us.

Sherlock Holmes took in the gloomy space at a glance. "I take it there is no electric lighting as yet?"

"Electricity is scheduled in Notting Hill and Holland Park for early next year."

"I see. And what has become of the post?"

"I put it on his desk." She pointed to a small alcove in which a plain desk of stained oak had been inserted.

"Watson, would you do the honors?" Holmes gestured to the desk where I sifted rapidly through a clutch of bills from various unremarkable quarters, patent medicine circulars, and subscriptions to several art periodicals.

"There doesn't seem to be anything here in the nature of personal correspondence," I noted. "Merely bills, invoices, and circulars from familiar sources."

He peered over my shoulder. "Just the sort of thing expected to accumulate in one's absence," he murmured. "Though further scrutiny may yield additional lines of inquiry."

Without additional comment, he pulled open the drawers and peered into their recesses.

"Hullo, this is curious."

"What have you found?" I asked.

"Nothing. These drawers are conspicuously empty. I would call that curious." He turned to Lady Glendenning, who waited expectantly. "What do you know of Rupert Milestone, Lady Glendenning?"

She offered an exasperated sigh. "Not a great deal, I'm afraid. Only his reputation."

"Not where he is from? Nothing about his people?"

"Nothing, Mr. Holmes. Remember, I inherited him, as with many others, a tenant from my late husband. All I can state for a certainty is that he paid his rent on time. I think—" she hesitated, biting her lip, as if uncertain of what she was about to say.

"Yes?"

"I think I once heard him refer to a brother in Shropshire, but I may have misheard. I'm sorry I can't be more helpful."

"That fault is none of yours, Lady Glendenning. Tell me, how does Mr. Milestone pay his rent?"

"He sends checks drawn from his account at the Saxe-Coburg branch of The City and Suburban Bank.[*] They always arrive on the first of the month. Until recently, that is."

"I see."

"It is very cold," I remarked. "Is it possible to light the stove in the corner?"

She shook her head. "I'm afraid that is not a stove."

---

[*] Small world! This is the same bank and branch where Holmes foiled a robbery by the ingenious John Clay in *"The Adventure of the Red-Headed League."*

"Oh?" Holmes moved closer to inspect the object, which, despite its imposing dimensions, took up very little space in the huge room. "This is a kiln," he declared.

"It is," Lady Glendenning agreed.

"A kiln?" I was not sure I'd heard correctly.

"A furnace built to bake and glaze ceramics such as are turned on a potter's wheel." The detective's store of miscellaneous knowledge never ceased to amaze me. "The trick," he went on, "is maintaining an even degree of heat, though I note this kiln has not been used in some time. Like all else, it wears a mantle of dust. In addition, I note the gas pipe that feeds it has been disconnected." Holmes gestured to the valve.

"I never noticed that," Lady Glendenning said, "though now I think of it, on none of my visits do I recall seeing it in use. And now you've drawn my attention to it, we've received no bills for the gas here for months."

"May I retain this?" Reaching within the oven, Holmes extracted a piece of scorched cloth no bigger than a place mat, holding it to the faint light to reveal a burnt square at its center.

The landlady frowned. "If you like."

Folding the stiff material gently, Holmes pocketed the square. He made no further comment but concluded his inspection of the massive porcelain device. Indifferent to the cold, he shed his greatcoat and commenced prowling the studio inch by inch, sniffing and employing his magnifier, emitting a series of whistles, yelps, and growls, reminiscent of a hound on the scent. Our client was evidently startled by the detective's behavior but I had beheld it often.

The atelier contained very little. Standing like an island in the midst of its cathedral-like immensity was an easel supporting a large canvas, presently concealed by a drop cloth.

"May I?" Holmes asked, one hand holding a corner of the cloth.

"As you please," responded Lady Glendenning.

Holmes drew off the cloth, revealing a view of Venice. I had never visited that picturesque location myself, but I had seen enough depictions to recognize the place at once, though the lower half of the painting was incomplete.

"Saint Mark's Square?" Holmes had never mentioned visiting Venice but I assumed his knowledge, like mine, was derived from previous illustrations.

"I couldn't say, I'm sure," responded our client.

After gazing thoughtfully at the picture some moments more, Holmes replaced the drop cloth and looked about him. Propped against the walls on either side along the floor were smaller easels and numerous pictures, some seemingly complete and others evidently works in progress, though in the gloom it was difficult to make them out. Above these, hanging by their corners on nails unceremoniously hammered into the wall, was a collection of picture frames of varied shapes and sizes, some rectangular, others square, still others oval or circular. Some were ornate and gilded; others plain and fashioned from bleached wood or what, on closer examination, proved to be papier-mâché.

In the center of the room, a mobile tray on casters contained an array of utensils, brushes of varying thickness, and colourful paint tubes, the pigments haphazardly squeezed in different combinations onto a large palette next to a blunt-ended palette knife. The odor of linseed oil and turpentine, as Lady Glendenning foretold, was not unpleasant.

At the room's eastern end were knocked-up crude shelves of white pine containing blank canvases on stretchers, awaiting the painter's brush.

I now became aware of another smell, familiar, but by no means as agreeable. It vexed me that I couldn't place it.

Near the large easel was a dark wooden, throne-like chair of gothic aspect, the back perforated with fleur-de-lis and a pointed arch. Behind the chair stood a black and gold folding screen, calling to mind the oriental screens on either side of Houdini's brick wall. Flung carelessly over the chair's high back was a bolt of purple satin. Beside it was a small table crowded with jugs and vases (one hosting a long-dead arrangement of sunflowers), along with beer steins, pewter plates, a stuffed peacock, and some fake lemons. I knew the fruits to be artificial as they would have mildewed by this time if the studio had indeed been vacant for as long as our client stipulated. I speculated this miscellaneous collection were props variously employed to enhance the painter's compositions.

Clustered in the vicinity of the easel on the floor were splattered drops and globules of paint. To these, the detective appeared to be paying particular attention, hovering over the specks with his magnifier. As I observed his actions, I could hardly miss what he was studying; a cluster of footprints imprinted in the paint splatches. At one point, to my surprise, he sucked in a deep breath and blew forcefully at the multicoloured collage before clambering to his feet.

"And now the pictures," he said, drawing closer to the walls where the canvases lay stacked. "May we have more light?"

Silently, Lady Glendenning lit additional gas jets, enabling us to peer more closely at the works.

While there were some seascapes, cityscapes, and still lifes (the lemons and sunflowers), most were portraits of sitters I did not recognize and, of these, most were attractive women. I could not fail to notice how the props I had seen crowded on the table were redistributed among the paintings in order to complement their subjects. I saw pewter plates and vases with flowers in endless combinations. One particularly colourful woman swathed in pink satin was juxtaposed with the peacock and its splayed emerald tail feathers.

Holmes made no comment as he knelt from one canvas to the next. The pictures struck me as professional but I am no expert. Were I called upon to elaborate, all I could say is that they were agreeable yet somehow familiar. Why I felt and what I meant by this I was unable to articulate.

Finally Holmes rose to his feet, brushing off his knees. "And the living quarters?" He had completed his tour of the studio.

These proved more impressive than we had been led to believe. They were of modest dimensions, yet it was evident the artist lived quite comfortably here. There was a small but sufficient kitchen with an empty kettle on the wood-burning stove beside the basin, tap, and larder, though no food was in evidence and the oven, when I opened it, contained nothing but undisturbed ashes.

The artist was evidently accustomed to taking most of his meals elsewhere.

As Holmes inspected the bathroom with its tin hip bath, I peered into the wardrobe.

"His clothes look to be in order," I remarked, and to be sure, neither the wardrobe nor the bureau bore signs of alteration or disturbance. On the contrary, a profusion of varied and costly attire was neatly arranged, more suited to a gentleman of means than what I imagined would comprise a painter's apparel. Crammed on the floor beside the wardrobe was a dark oak linen chest.

"I infer Mr. Milestone does well," said Holmes, reading my thoughts as he inspected hangers in the open wardrobe. "There are labels here from Savile Row. Excepting the paint-splattered clogs the painter evidently wore while working, the shoes are bespoke from Canons and there are several pairs in differing styles."

"I believe he is a member of the Garrick," said Lady Glendenning, behind us. "Which makes his nonpayment of rent the more puzzling," she added with some bitterness.

"Are you aware of any photographs? They might prove useful."

She shook her head. "I have never seen any." Then, struck by a thought, she added, "But there is something," before leading us into the artist's small but well-appointed bedroom and lighting the gas there.

"Is this also one of Mr. Milestone's?" The detective gestured to the portrait of a strikingly handsome individual over the mantelpiece at the foot of the artist's large bed. Even to my untutored eye, I could see that the aggressive strong-jawed face, broad forehead, high cheekbones, piercing dark eyes, and sensuous mouth were not the work of the same painter. The golden locks framing the pale brow above them proclaimed an Adonis.

"It is not." The lady seemed to hesitate. "It was painted by Burne-Jones and is a likeness of Mr. Milestone himself."

"Most convenient," Holmes quizzed the painting. "A face to remember. Does it do him justice, would you say?"

Again, our client appeared flustered. "I think it does," she finally answered in a low tone. "Though this appears to have been done some time ago."

Holmes raised his eyebrows. "Indeed. So . . . not a portrait of Dorian Gray?"

"I don't believe I know anyone of that name."

Holmes offered a dry laugh but chose not to reply as he continued to scrutinize the image.

"The man is wonderfully prepossessing," he acknowledged, stepping closer then back in the small space between the mantel and the foot of the bed. "One can perhaps imagine why so many of his sitters were of the fair sex. It must have been"—he hesitated over his choice of words—"tempting to sit for this painter."

Lady Glendenning said nothing to this.

After staring some moments longer at the picture, Holmes retrieved his coat. "Very well, Lady Glendenning. I think I've seen all I came to see, though my research may prompt my return at some later date."

"What do you think, Watson?"

We had finally emerged at the Edgware Road and, seeing my fatigue, the detective persuaded me to stop for a ploughman's lunch at the George & Dragon before trudging back to Baker Street. The fare was indifferent but filling and a whisky served to warm my insides and restore my spirits.

"Think?"

"About what we have seen. And smelled," he added. "The case presents features of interest, wouldn't you say?"

"What sort of features?"

The detective commenced soundlessly drumming his fingers on the tabletop. "The empty desk, for a start. Clearly it is there for the artist's use, a place to address bills, prepare invoices and other correspondence, the sort of household and professional obligations that relate to any man's life."

"But it was entirely empty."

"Entirely empty," he echoed. "What sort of desk is that, then? And what of the kiln? A kiln with no ceramics and no potter's wheel in sight. Empty save for this." He gently set down the blackened swatch of cloth he'd extracted from the kiln with its blistered square of what looked like paint at its center. "I believe this was once canvas," he said.

"Perhaps he gave up on ceramics," I hazarded, swallowing the last of my whisky. "He had the gas pipe capped at the kiln."

Holmes's fingers maintained their silent tattoo. "And the pumice stone?"

"What pumice stone?"

"Next to the paint brushes near the easel. I can understand a pumice stone near a wash basin for use on hands or feet, but what was one doing near the artist's palette?"

I frowned at this. "For all we know artists use all manner of tools to achieve their effects."

"Possibly." The detective's fingers did not cease their drumming. "And the pictures?"

"I'm no critic—" I began but he cut me off, waggling the cheese knife back and forth in an admonitory fashion.

"Come, come, Watson. Everyone is a critic, or, at any rate, has a right to their opinion. Surely you formed an opinion of Milestone's portraits?"

"I liked the women . . ."

"To be sure. You are a connoisseur. But. I hear a *but*."

I told him the impression I had formed of the pictures' vague sense of familiarity. I could swear I'd seen versions of that Venetian cityscape on more than one occasion.

"I see what you mean," he agreed. "One has seen those sorts of daubs many times in many places. I think it safe to say these fail to proclaim the individuality of the artist."

"I had not thought of it in that way."

"And what of the portrait by Burne-Jones?"

"Ah, yes, that was altogether remarkable."

"True, but did you make note of the picture's most arresting feature?"

"I'm not sure what you mean. The frame seemed—"

"The placement, Watson! The placement! The picture hangs on the wall at the foot of Milestone's bed! It would be the last thing the man saw before he closed his eyes and the first thing he beheld when he opened them."

"Well, when you put it that way, Milestone appears to be—"

"A trifle vain?" He tapped his mouth thoughtfully with his napkin. "Which brings us to the next item of interest, the nearby oak linen chest."

"What of it? Linen chests are common."

Holmes sat back and drained his pint, now blotting his lips with the back of his hand. "But who troubles to padlock a linen chest?"

"Was it padlocked? I didn't notice."

Holmes sighed but spared me the repetition of his homily. "And then there is the matter of the bathroom wash basin."

"What of it?" I recalled the hip bath but not the wash basin.

"There are a great many tawny-coloured shaving hairs in it."

"They surely correspond to the hairs in the portrait. What does that suggest? Other than the fact that he disdains a housekeeper."

"The hairs were rather long."

"Possibly he does not shave daily? The man's a painter, not a professor. If the spirit was upon him, such habits may go by the boards. He might work for days without stopping for a wash."

"Possibly. But where is the razor?"

"Holmes, be reasonable, we conducted a rapid search in dim light. It's possible you missed it."

It was clear Holmes was not mollified. "That just leaves the formaldehyde. . . ." he murmured.

"The—" I snapped my fingers. "Yes! That pungent odor! I knew I smelled something familiar but disagreeable. I couldn't place it. . . ."

"No more could I, until I found a tin of the stuff amongst Milestone's paint supplies. Have you not encountered a face you knew but couldn't name because it wasn't where you were accustomed to seeing it—at the tobacconist's till, behind the counter at the greengrocer's, or at the bar in a public house . . . ?

Formaldehyde—we've smelled that nauseating odor a hundred times, in funeral parlors and the like, but didn't recognize it out of its element, so to speak."

"What possible use could the man have for formaldehyde?" I was relieved to learn that I had not been alone in being unable to place the origins of that familiar scent.

"Indeed. Formaldehyde is used for embalming but it has other uses and characteristics. The human body produces it naturally. So do bananas, come to that. It is used in paint, to be sure, and glue"—Holmes, I needed no reminding, had begun his professional life as a chemist—"but that doesn't explain the phenol," he mused.

"The what?"

"Phenol. Another chemical I found among Mr. Milestone's supplies. It is sometimes used—"

"I'm a doctor, Holmes. I know what phenol is. I've prescribed it on occasion for sore throats."

"An antiseptic, then. That being the case, why do I find it among the artist's supplies? If he used it for an occasional sore throat, surely his medicine cupboard would make a more suitable location."

The detective fished out his pipe and began packing it with shag, a sure indication of introspection to come. I wondered whether it would prove a one-, two-, or three-pipe problem.

"So," he continued, pausing to enjoy the aroma emanating from the tobacco pouch, "we have a painter of competent, if arguably unoriginal canvases, who lives and dresses more than comfortably, yet fails to pay his rent."

"Perhaps he is indebted to his tailor as well. That could describe many a gentleman."

"It could. Though I'm not sure Mr. Milestone would qualify. Clothes don't make the man."

"You sound rather a snob, Holmes."

"Do I?" He shrugged. "We lionize artists, to be sure, but they are typically on the periphery of society. Even the great Beethoven was relegated to the servants' entrance." He leaned forward, lowering his voice. "What we have here, Watson, is a very queer set of digs. An empty desk, a kiln with no potting wheel or ceramics, an unfinished Venetian cityscape, a pumice stone beside an easel rather than a wash basin, a padlocked linen chest, an oddly situated portrait of the artist as a young man, shaving hairs in the sink, but no razor, a wardrobe more suited to Mayfair than Notting Hill—and at least one mysterious chemical."

I marveled at the detective's ability to keep every scrap of our findings in his head, but felt the need to contribute to our store of knowledge.

"All covered with dust."

"Precisely. Very good, Watson."

"Holmes, what do you think has happened? Is it possible that for some reason we have yet to determine, Rupert Milestone has bolted? Fled somewhere? The Continent? South America? That would explain his empty desk—he wished to avoid leaving behind incriminating documents. Perhaps he burned the lot in the kitchen stove. That might explain all those ashes."

The detective shook his head and signaled for the reckoning. "It is unwise to draw conclusions prematurely," he advised in his oracular mode, "but I think it highly unlikely."

"But the man was behind on his rent! Perhaps he had overspent on his Savile Row attire and other indulgences, resulting in additional financial—"

"I'm afraid it won't do, Watson." Half standing, Holmes dug deep into his trouser pocket and produced a fistful of fifty-pound notes. It was all I could do to refrain from whistling. "Rupert Milestone has plenty of money, enough to pay his rent *and* his tailor. I found these stuffed into the toe of one of a pair of tasseled brogues and, had I time, I would not have been astonished to find more. Those who squirrel money away in one place invariably stash it in others, oftentimes forgetting where." He shoved the banknotes back into his pocket. "Even assuming a man of the sort we glimpsed in his portrait would flee the country leaving behind his extraordinary wardrobe, what on earth could induce a man on the run to abandon his nest eggs? I wager we'll find his bank accounts untouched as well. No, Watson, there is more to this affair than a painter behind on his rent."

I had to acknowledge my friend's reasoning. "But if the man was not in financial straits, why begrudge paying his rent?"

He smiled. "Another enigma, Watson. Lady Glendenning has presented us with something badly needed."

"A miracle?"

"One can always hope."

"But what about your notion that there may be some mundane explanation for all we have seen? Remember Norbury."

The detective's features briefly clouded over at my allusion to one of his infrequent failures.* But he shook his head like a dog sloughing off water and, recovering his poise, gazed in my direction, his gray eyes bright. "There is a final detail that may also have escaped your notice."

"What detail?" I had followed his inspection of the artist's studio attentively.

"You recall the floor near the easel was splattered with a good deal of paint."

"What of it? Surely that is to be—"

"Not all of it was paint, Watson. A deal of it—a very great deal, I'm afraid—was dried blood."

The miracle had arrived.

---

* *The Adventure of the Yellow Face*—a case in which Holmes added up the clues, concocted a theory that fit all the facts, only to learn that his conclusion was entirely mistaken.

3

ELIMINATING THE IMPOSSIBLE

The chatter and clatter of the George & Dragon subsided as if all sound had been sucked from the taproom.

"Are you sure it was blood?" My voice sounded louder than I intended.

"Quite sure." The detective's glittering eyes bored into mine. "As you know, years before we met, I was living near the British Museum where I spent my days in the Reading Room, devouring the data in that extraordinary repository. There I hoped to increase the knowledge that would ultimately bear on my calling."

"I recollect your saying that you sat in Karl Marx's old chair?"

He smiled. "So I was told. In any event, during the course of my research I stumbled upon the curious properties of oil paint, which, as I learned, takes an eternity to dry. Art is not my province, as you know, but chemistry is and so I read on, storing away miscellaneous information on the subject. One never knows what might prove useful. I even went so far as to consult a specialist who demonstrated a simple test for the age of such paint."

"And that is?"

"To insert a pin into a sample of what is on the canvas. The outer layer of paint may appear hard but twirl the pin underneath and the soft inside that has not yet congealed will allow a rough estimate as to when the paint was first applied." He sat back, releasing my eyes from his steadfast gaze. "A soft interior might be justified if the painting in question were new, less than fifty years old, let us say, but if the picture was presented as almost three hundred, the paint both outside and in should have hardened like stone."

"I'm not sure I—"

"Those parti-hued splotches on Milestone's studio floor are recent and sticky. They would not allow me to blow off the dust that had settled on them, no matter how hard I puffed, whereas the motes on the brown gouts among them allowed me to disperse the dust with a single breath. Blood dries much faster than paint."

I tried to think but was so astonished by his words that I had difficulty marshaling my thoughts. "It's a wonder I did not see the blood."

"You saw what you expected to see, my dear fellow, splotches of paint near an artist's easel. The devil is always in the details."

"Ought we to inform the police?" was the best I could manage.

To my surprise the detective appeared hesitant. A slender forefinger played with water rings on the table.

"I think not," said he at length. Seeing my look, he went on. "I fail to see that we owe the police anything at this juncture. Lady Glendenning went to them for a start and her pleas were ignored. Gregson and his crew of bumblers couldn't even be bothered to visit Milestone's studio. I believe we have first claim on what we found there. Or failed to find," he added. "I feel no compunction to share my conclusions, especially without evidence."

I was not entirely convinced by this line of reasoning. "What about our client? Oughtn't we to tell her?"

"That is a point that ought to be considered," the detective said in a tone that indicated he had already considered it. "I think for the moment we will maintain the status quo. What we found is incomplete, to say the least. We note incongruities, we cite anomalies, and infer the likelihood of a crime, but that is all."

"But there is the blood."

"That is so."

"Then what will you do?"

He sat back and signaled for the reckoning as the pub's cacophony reasserted itself. "I expect we must wait for the snow to melt."

I drew back in surprise. "What's that you say?"

"Think, Watson. The strong likelihood is that a man has been killed in Rupert Milestone's atelier. Provisionally, let us assume it was a man, not a woman, or a cow. The crime was spontaneous."

"How can you possibly know that?"

"Because the killer chose an inconvenient time of year to dispose of his victim. There were two sets of bespoke footwear in all that paint mess near the easel. Square toes were made by Canons and likely belonged to the painter as he had others of the same make."

"And the other pair?"

He sat back and sniffed the air. "The other pair, pointed toes, were made by Kirbys, if I judge the prints aright. Mind you, in that slithery mishmash my observations must remain interim. Pointed toes belonged to Milestone's visitor. Their altercation began with Pointed Toes pacing back and forth near but not close to the easel. Pacing implies agitation of some kind . . ." He trailed off, lost in thought.

"And then?" I found myself almost breathless, waiting for the detective's account as if he were an eyewitness.

"In the struggle that followed, the combatants closed in on each other and paint splotches on the floor were smeared by their footwear as they danced into a full-blown confrontation, at which point Square Toes and Pointed Toes were literally toe to toe. Interim," he repeated.

"We didn't see any paint on the shoes in Milestone's wardrobe, only on his clogs."

"Which he evidently preferred while working. But he was not painting when his visitor arrived."

"Do you think he was anticipating his visitor?"

Holmes hesitated. "He might have been."

"So," I urged, "the blood arguably belongs to one or the other of the combatants."

"Possibly both, doctor."

During the silence that followed as we considered this possibility, another thought occurred to me. "You said the killer chose an inconvenient time of year. What did you mean by that?"

"Only that if the murder had been premeditated, the murderer would have made a plan to conceal the remains beforehand. The blizzard posed unanticipated difficulties for him."

"Why trouble to conceal the remains at all? Why not simply abandon the body where it fell?"

Holmes frowned at this and for a moment I was pleased by the notion that I had raised an objection he had not anticipated. But he soon brightened.

"For the simple reason that too many knew of bad blood that existed between both men. The death of one would inevitably cast suspicion on the part of the other. Hiding the victim would at least serve to postpone discovery of the crime, by which time the assailant would have made good his escape. Indeed, he may already have done so. No," he shook his head, "the killer was obliged to hide his sudden crime but was confronted by the unforeseen difficultly posed by the weather. Besides which, premeditation would not have envisioned a struggle, the outcome of which the assailant could not assure. What happened in that studio took both men by surprise. Angry words were spoken that abruptly turned to blows. And finally blood was shed. A great deal of blood," he repeated.

"Brilliant."

Holmes tried to conceal his pleasure. Vanity was his besetting sin. "As the death occurred, you might say, out of season, the killer was obliged to improvise. The blood on the floor might plausibly be mistaken for paint—which indeed you did—but what was to be done with the body? That is the question! In this frozen tundra he can't have buried it hereabouts, nor, with the roads as they are, could he have transported it far. Burned it in the kiln perhaps, but that runs the risk of a suspicious stench. Much of the Thames is presently frozen, making it both conspicuous and problematic to wander onto literally thin ice with a parcel whose dead weight—you will forgive the expression—can only increase the risk of cracking the surface, drowning both victor and vanquished. And if the corpse itself were not properly weighted, it would likely resurface."

"Holmes, I've just eaten . . ."

"These possibilities must be considered, Watson! The body may well have been dismembered, but even so, dispersal of the parts poses a difficulty." He tossed some coins on the table. "I postulate a snowdrift presented the simplest expedient. If that theory holds, we find ourselves obliged to wait for a thaw."

Here was yet another cheerful thought. "And in the meantime?"

Holmes knocked his pipe bowl against the ashtray. "In the meantime, I should like to know more about Rupert Milestone and why he was attempting to glaze a square of paint in his kiln. I think a visit to Pall Mall is in order."

"Mycroft?"

"My brother's command of arcana improbably exceeds my own. We've not seen each other since the onset of these snowfalls. I think it as good an excuse as any to pay a call and see how he is getting on."

"Will you find him at the Diogenes?"

"I can't imagine finding him anywhere else. Come," said he, rising, "let us return to Baker Street and set you down before a cozy fire."

Holmes, who was fond of describing himself as a thinking machine, a brain with the rest as mere appendage, was, in reality, a devoted friend. His skittishness where emotions were concerned ("emotion clouds logic," he cautioned on more than one occasion), lent an added piquancy to those moments when strong feelings broke through his fortifications of reserve. Getting me back to Baker Street after our day's travails was one such occasion. It was only after helping me into my dressing gown and setting my feet in a bowl of hot water, a rum toddy within reach, that he ceased his ministrations and expressed his intention of leaving once again.

"So soon? Holmes you must be tired yourself."

"I will be tired later, my dear fellow, but, as I've noted, winter isn't the only thing hereabouts that is getting colder by the minute. I'll slip into dry clothes and have a word with Mrs. Hudson on my way out. Ring her if you need anything and I will make it my business to keep you apprised of developments."

So saying, he closed the door behind him, leaving me to my rum and ruminations. I was exhausted but somehow too tired to sleep. Dully aware of the cooling water at my ankles, I stared at the fire, hypnotized by its pulsing glow as I nursed my drink, trying to make sense of the strange affair in which we had become involved. In my notebook, I jotted Holmes's summary as I recalled it:

> *An empty desk.*
> *A kiln with neither potting wheel nor ceramics, but a square of bubbling paint on a singed canvas within.*
> *An unfinished painting of Venice.*

A pumice stone that appears to have strayed from the bath and wash basin.
A padlocked linen chest.
An oddly situated portrait of the artist.
Shaved hairs in the wash basin with no razor in sight.
A wardrobe more suited to Pall Mall than Notting Hill.
Square toes from Canons and pointed toes from Kirbys.
One anomalous chemical.
A great deal of blood.

To this I added a layer of dust and Rupert Milestone's profusion of hidden banknotes, capped by the detective's assertion that an unexpected killing had taken place.

I must have dozed off for when I woke it was dark, the fire now embers, and someone—in all likelihood Mrs. Hudson—had removed the bowl of water from beneath my feet and draped me in a counterpane down to my toes. As I shuffled wearily off to bed, blanketed like a squaw, I noted that Holmes had not returned.

When I woke, much refreshed the following morning, the sun was blazing and the sky a brilliant blue, an astonishing transformation after weeks of unceasing gray. Mrs. Hudson had silently laid on a breakfast, the contents still warm beneath chafing dishes, but there was no sign of Holmes and his bed had not been slept in. I was not entirely surprised by this. Oftentimes on a case, the detective might disappear for days on end and he had begun his trip to the Diogenes late the day before. I contented myself with the meal before me, relishing strong black coffee, bacon and scones as I perused *The Globe*. More trouble appeared to be brewing in the Sudan but I saw nothing that might pertain to recent events in Notting Hill.

I spent the morning arranging my notes of the case thus far, hoping that laying them out in the broad light of day might make matters clearer, but reread the results finding myself no better than before. Why would a man with ready access to cash fail to pay his rent? If he had decamped, for whatever reason, why leave behind the means to aid and sustain his flight? It was then that I was struck by a dark thought. Eliminate the impossible, Holmes was fond of declaring, and the remainder, by whatever name, must be the truth. The detective had concluded a sudden struggle had occurred. Was it not then possible that Rupert Milestone was the victim of that altercation? That might account for his disappearance and abandoning his money. If this were so, it followed that the killer had no inkling his victim secreted funds about the place or surely he would have searched for them and helped himself. Or possibly, as events had taken him by surprise, he had to move quickly and lacked the time? He emptied the desk against the possibility that incriminating correspondence identifying him by name might be found and fled.

But what had become of the body? Was it possible the man had not died? Staggered off somehow and eluded his assailant? I shook my head at the thought; not with the loss of so much blood.

I was unable to theorize past this point. Who might his assailant be? Whoever it was could afford shoes from Kirbys. Holmes had posited there was ill will between the victim and his assailant, likely known to several. He had also speculated that women might have been eager to pose for the "prepossessing" painter. Could

Milestone's killer be the disgruntled lover or husband of one of the painter's subjects? I remembered Holmes's dictum that one cannot make bricks without clay. I lacked sufficient data to explore the possibility. To answer the question, would one first need to identify and interview each of those attractive sitters? The prospect of such interrogations prompted an involuntary sigh.

By noon, with still no sign of the detective, I fell to rearranging notes of previous cases in which the detective had played a part, hoping that by revisiting his methods, I might see some light. I had exhausted this diversion when Mrs. Hudson bustled in with a fresh tray, insisting we open a window if only for ten minutes to air out our rooms. I surrendered to her reasoning that the place had become unhygienic, dined gratefully after the window was shut again, then sat in my chair, intending to pass the time with one of Rider Haggard's novels of the Zulu wars.

It had just gone three when Holmes returned, ruddy-faced and breathless. "I'm famished," he announced without preamble, kicking off his snow-soaked shoes and tucking into the remains of my lunch, not troubling to remove his coat. He was in want of a shave and dressed in the same clothes he wore when he left. In a few words, I outlined my tentative theory that the painter had been the victim.

"Bravo, Watson. Yours is certainly a theory that covers the facts so far as we know them."

I endeavored to conceal my pleasure at these rare words of approbation, inwardly acknowledging that, on occasion, I was as capable of vanity as my friend. Instead, I implored him to continue his narrative. "Holmes, I'm all ears. What have you learned?"

He held up a hand to forestall talk, allowing him to swallow his last mouthful before sitting back with a sigh. "A great deal, Watson. A very great deal. I've yet to understand how useful any of it may be, but I have certainly received an education."

"On what subject?"

"Art, my dear fellow. Or rather, the business of art. For, as it turns out, art of late has become a big and profitable business. When I left you, I made my way to the Diogenes in search of Mycroft. No matter how many times over the years I've set foot in the place, its eccentricities continue to baffle me."

"I seem to remember that talking is forbidden except in the Strangers' Room."

"Even there it is not encouraged! Unlike the convivial Garrick, the genially depraved Whites and others of that ilk, the Diogenes is a club for members who despise clubs and caters to those who see and prefer themselves as solitaries. I believe Gibbon was a member. At all events, Harcourt, who knows me by now, set down a tray of tea and éclairs and went reluctantly in search of Mycroft, who appeared none too pleased to see me. 'I am very busy, Sherlock,' were his words of greeting. More corpulent than ever, he was brushing crumbs from his waistcoat, but following my look, declared, 'Even the British government has to eat. Why have you suddenly become interested in Renoir, as I note from the catalogue protruding from your coat pocket? I am dealing with a crisis.' Naturally, I had no idea what crisis he was talking about."

"Something to do with the Sudan, I'll wager." The detective raised his eyebrows at this. "It was in the papers, Holmes."

"It does not bear on our investigation," was his only comment before resuming his account. "As time was important, I outlined the case to my brother without identifying any of the principals, and asked him what he knew about Bond Street, where, as you are doubtless aware, many picture galleries are located.

"'Art is a funny business,' Mycroft began, helping himself to one of my éclairs. 'There are no rules.'

"'Rather like life?' I offered.

"'Sherlock, you're never quite as amusing as you fancy yourself.'

"'I apologize. Whom should I consult?'

"He passed a massive hand over his mouth. 'Well, there's Christie's in King Street, of course, but they are mainly an auction house. Sotheby, Wilkinson, & Hodge is more or less the same thing, but if you really want to know about your vanished painter, you might just as well begin at the top.'

"'The top being—?'

"'Van Dam's.' Seeing my bewildered look, he heaved an exasperated sigh. 'Surely you've heard of Sir Jonathan Van Dam, lately Lord Southbank, the most important art dealer in the world. One might add, notorious. Van Dam's is newer than Christie's or Sotheby's but larger than both combined. While the man's Walloon* background seems a little murky, there's no doubting Sir Jonathan has turned the trade in pictures into a vast enterprise, with many imitators following in his oversized footsteps. My dear Sherlock, you really must consent to visit Earth every now and again.'

---

* French-speaking Belgians from the southern and eastern portions of that small country.

"'I promise, Mycroft, at the very first opportunity. Tell me about Sir Jonathan.'

"'No one calls him that. The amiable Lord Southbank is known everywhere as Sir Johnny. Van Dam's boasts palatial offices in Piccadilly—you've surely remarked on them—also in Paris at the Place Vendôme and in New York somewhere on the Fifth Avenue. Sir Johnny specializes in old masters, but I daresay casts a wider net, should the occasion demand it.'

"'Old masters?'

"'Are you going to eat that?'

"'Help yourself, Mycroft. What old masters are we talking about?'

"'European painting up to the start of the eighteenth century, were I to hazard a guess.'

"'Which you enjoined me from infancy never to do, Mycroft.'

"'Must you always have the last word, Sherlock?'

"'So sorry. Do go on.'

"Mycroft glared at me as if wondering whether to oblige, then gave it up, judging further argument too much bother. As you know, my brother tends to lethargy.

"'Sir Johnny's worldwide emporia deal almost exclusively in old masters and of course the only old masters worth owning are the ones *he* sells. And, as old masters do not grow on trees, you may imagine he does a brisk business. The man has assiduously founded museums everywhere on behalf of countries and captains of industry looking to enshrine their names on metropolitan enterprises. In New York, in Washington, and of course, the shiny new Tate on the Embankment. By now these places are cherished institutions, eagerly patronized by the public and ensuring Sir Johnny's place as all the Medici rolled into one. The man's much given to blarney but he is a salesman *par excellence*. Why, there was a story told not so very long ago that when Lord Etherington—'

"'The press baron?'

"'The same. When Etherington announced his intention of acquiring art, of course everyone told him, "Why, then you must see Sir Johnny," and so he duly turned up in Piccadilly, where he was welcomed by the great man in his sumptuous office. There they sat chatting for three hours about everything under the sun—except art.'

"'Why would Sir J—?'

"'If you'll show a little patience, Sherlock. When the tycoon ventured to bring up the purpose of his visit, the old scoundrel smacked his forehead and apologized. "Forgive me! Here you've come to look at pictures and all we've done is pass the time of day. If you'll just follow me, I've set aside some wonderful canvases I think you would do well to start off with—"

"'How could Sir Johnny have already set aside—'

"Mycroft shrugged his ursine shoulders. 'I've had the story at secondhand but the outcome is now legend. Etherington followed his host up stairs that would have done credit to the palace at Schönbrunn and they passed through a room in which the black velvet–draped walls were stuffed with Rembrandts.'

"'Rembrandts.'

"'The master of old masters. The art collector's Holy Grail! Even ignoramuses recognize him on sight. Eight Rembrandts, mark you, but Sir Johnny paid them no heed, heading for the farther door as if they didn't exist, when Etherington stopped and pointed.

"I say, aren't these Rembrandts?"

"'Yes,' answered the art dealer, "but—"

"If they're Rembrandts why aren't we discussing these?" Etherington wondered.

"They're sold," Van Dam explained quickly. "Now if you'll just step this way—"

"But if they're sold, why are they still here?" persisted the press baron. Sir Johnny shrugged dismissively.

"Just a few minor contractual details to be concluded, but in this next room—"

"But if the contracts are not concluded," Etherington doggedly pursued, "then these Rembrandts are still in your possession?"

"Technically," Van Dam sighed and admitted, "but—"

"Then why cannot I bid on them?" Etherington wanted to know. "My money is surely as good as Duke so-and-so's."

"Look here, this is rather awkward," returns Sir Johnny. "I believe these pictures are somewhat beyond your price range. Now if you'll just accompany me to the next room, what I've selected for you is just—"

"Beyond my price range!" exclaimed the indignant client—'

"Mycroft sat back, smiling. 'Of course, you know the sequel. There was no next room, or at any rate nothing worth mentioning within it. And before you could say Jack Robinson, Sir Johnny had unloaded eight—eight!—priceless Rembrandts on the neophyte art collector.'

"'Interesting,' I allowed.

"'Or he'll call on a Rothschild who has assured him in no uncertain terms that he is not buying this year and say, "That presents no difficulty, your lordship, as I've nothing to sell, but as it happens I've a painting I've no room to store. Would you hold on to it as a favor for a time? Stash it anywhere, there's a good fellow." With that line of patter he'll let a year pass before calling the man to reclaim it. By this time, his gull will have fallen hopelessly in love with the picture and its attractive subject, and rather than returning, insist on buying it. And there, in a word or two, you have Sir Johnny, distilled.'"

Holmes sat back, smiling in the fashion of his brother.

"Well, I had to own those tales were eye-openers, Watson, but now a new thought occurred to me. 'And just how could a swell like Lord Etherington be sure of what he was paying for? Eight Rembrandts! How could the man be certain he was getting the real thing?'

"Mycroft favored me with a look of fraternal disdain. 'Dear boy, older paintings must be authenticated. With modern art, the so-called pre-Raphaelites and those scoffed as "Impressionists," the question does not arise, but to pay thousands for a Caravaggio or a Titian and be sure of its worth requires the services of a qualified authenticator, one who can distinguish wheat from chaff. The history of art is also the history of fraud. Do you know the origin of the word *sincere*?'

"'Must I?'

"Mycroft was unruffled. 'Its etymology might give you some idea of the world you propose to enter, where chicanery is as common as counterfeiting. *Sincere* comes from the Latin: *sine*—without or lacking—and *cere*—wax. Sin-cere. Without wax.'

"'And this pertains to fakery how?' I asked wearily.

"'Let us say you are an ancient Roman who wishes to purchase a marble statue—'

"I heaved a sigh, Watson, for once on his podium, my brother was in no hurry to leave it. 'Let us say it,' I agreed. 'I am an elderly Roman.'

"'And someone has an attractive statue you rather fancy,' he returned. 'The marble is wonderfully smooth.'

"'Mycroft—'

"'Only it isn't smooth!' My brother sat forward, suddenly animated, having arrived at the point of his disquisition. 'It isn't smooth at all! In fact, it has been chipped and dinged in several places! But the damage has been, one might say, artfully concealed by *rubbing wax* into all the crevices and fissures so as to render them invisible to our gullible collector! What the collector truly hopes for is a smooth statue, *minus wax*: "sin-cere!" For this our acquisitive Roman requires the services of an authenticator, as have collectors of statues and pictures ever since.'

"'I take it the statue I have purchased will not be left in broad sunlight, where melting wax might give away the game,' I could not help remarking, but Mycroft made a motion with his paw, brushing off my levity as if shooing a fly. 'I believe in London the last word on the subject of authentic Renaissance art and old masters is pronounced by a Signor Garibaldi. If memory serves he is exclusively in the employ of Van Dam's and his word is final.'"*

---

* Professor Ennio Garibaldi received his doctorate from the University of Padua in 1883, published *Italian Painters of Umbria* in 1885, and began continuous employment with Van Dam's in 1892.

"'You've been a font of information—as usual,' I told my brother. 'Tomorrow I believe I shall pay a call on Sir Johnny.'

"At which point Mycroft surprised me with a parting piece of advice. 'Don't go in your own persona, Sherlock. Art dealers are not fond of questions that do not pertain to pictures and profit.'

"'I carry a variety of visiting cards for such occasions,' I assured him and so took my leave. The last I saw when I turned to look, my brother was studying the remaining éclair as though it was a visiting card of its own. By this time it was too late to visit Lord Southbank's Piccadilly emporium so I put up at the Northumberland."

"Such extravagance," I teased.

"Our client can well afford it." Holmes continued eating. It was a perpetual wonder the man never put on weight whereas his brother was unable to remove it. "I put out my boots, hoping some overnight resuscitation was possible, but look at them now." He made a disparaging click with his tongue. "The drudgery of detective work has made me the cobblers' patron saint."

"Do march a straight line, Holmes. What happened at Van Dam's?"

"Van Dam's, it turns out, doesn't open its doors until eleven, so I began my day with a breakfast at Simpson's. Their kidney pie remains unsurpassed. The weather is warming and scrapers had largely cleared the remaining slush by the time I tromped down Park Lane and entered Piccadilly. I marveled that I never troubled to notice Van Dam's before. Its facade combines aspects of the Parthenon crossed with the Great Wall of China, a design that almost defies one to describe, much less ignore."

"I seem to recall passing it," I admitted.

"I must have done so dozens of times but was typically preoccupied with other matters. At all events, the interior was yet more imposing than its perplexing front. One finds oneself in an atrium as large and long as the Burlington Arcade but nearly twice again as high. All covered with pictures, mind you. There was a front desk that would have done credit to Napoleon's sepulcher at Invalides, behind which presided a monocled greeter with the posture of a grenadier.

"'May I be of service?' he inquired. He looked to be in early middle age with a touch of gray at his pomaded temples and spoke with an hauteur just short of condescension, implying that while he had better things to do—doubtless exchanging art chit-chat with today's Medici—yet he deigned to spare a few moments for hoi polloi such as myself.

"'I wish to speak with Sir Johnny on a most important matter,' I began in my best American and handed him my visiting card, which he squinted at through his monocle.

"'Jasper Gilmore, Topeka, Kansas,' he read aloud, glancing from the card to me.

"'I am the purchasing agent for Hezekiah Wilson,' I explained. 'Likewise of Topeka. Mr. Wilson wishes me to consult with Sir Johnny regarding the works of Rupert Milestone.'

"'Who?'

"'The painter.' I tried not to appear surprised by this inauspicious response. 'Mr. Wilson is an ardent admirer and wishes to acquire some of Milestone's—'

"'You've just missed Lord Southbank, Mister, uh—'

"'Gilmore. Where might I run him down? I'd greatly like to—'

"'Lord Southbank left for Paris this morning, and here at Van Dam's we deal only in old masters,' the man interrupted me smoothly. He was evidently accustomed to interrupting.

"'Paris,' I pursued. 'When will he return? I should very much like to meet him—I was referred by Julian Etherington. I am stopping at the Athenaeum.'

"For the first time the grenadier appeared uncertain. The double-barreled name of the newspaper tycoon and the well-known club penetrated his condescension, but he rallied—'I have no way of knowing, Mr. uh, Gilmore. Lord Southbank is very . . . peripatetic.'

"'Peri—?'

"'Lord Southbank seldom stays in one place for long as he has many interests to attend to.'

"'Is that him?' I gestured to the forbidding portrait behind the grenadier. I knew perfectly well it was as I had seen that lowering face caricatured on more than one occasion in *Punch* without knowing its owner by name. The founder of Van Dam's was a man in his midforties with tawny, leonine hair almost the same colour as the gilt frame that encompassed his image. His beard bristled with the energy and determination that the *Punch* cartoonists had caught so well. He looked altogether a specimen to be reckoned with.

"'It is.'"

"'Burne-Jones?' I took a stab, for the image somehow put me in mind of the portrait of Milestone in his bedroom.

"The grenadier stiffened. 'By no means. Gerome.'

"'Ah, yes, Gerome, to be sure. Recent?'

"'Painted some time ago.'

"'Ah,' said I once more. 'Gerome, to be sure. Perhaps another time.'

"With this I took my leave. I confess I did not know what to make of these data. Assuming Lady Glendenning had not exaggerated or been misinformed as to Milestone's reputation, how is it this factotum professed no knowledge of the man? And was it my imagination or did the grenadier seem uncertain as to his master's whereabouts?"

"All this cannot have taken long. Where did you go next?"

He shrugged. "In for a penny, Watson. I marched 'round to Bond Street and introduced myself to a Mr. Brudenell, general manager at the Rothermede Gallery."

"Another grenadier?"

"Cut from a different cloth, let us say. The man was shorter, in his early thirties, with an effete manner accentuated by a slight lisp, a delicate moustache, and what I judged to be an indifferently persuasive toupee. His speech hinted at formative years in Leeds or Hull. There was nothing in his bearing that suggested previous military employment but, at some point, he had engaged in a good deal of manual labor for his right-hand thumb and the heel of the palm were greatly calloused and larger than that of his left. As he stood behind a counter, I was denied the privilege of inspecting his knees. As you know, the hands, knees, and feet can provide vital information. But in contrast to the tight-lipped host at Van Dam's, Mr. Brudenell was loquacious, eager to impart knowledge and opinions.

"'Milestone? "Prince Rupert," the ladies term him. Yes, we know of him to be sure, but we do not show him. The first of the second-raters. The poor man's Sargent, as he's sometimes called.'

"'Sargent?'

"His pale forehead creased slightly at my ignorance but Mr. Brudenell was doubtless accustomed to it and answered with patience. 'John Singer Sargent, the American genius, famed worldwide for his portraits of the well-to-do, with the portraitist's invaluable gift of making his sitters appear more attractive than perhaps they are. Milestone's portraits may be said to fall into much the same category, but—how shall I put this?—while the brushwork is superlative, especially his rendering of satin and flesh tones, the totality remains somehow—' he hesitated, desirous, at the last moment, to appear tactful—'less memorable.'

"'I see.'

"'Both display a certain erotic charge, though with the exception of Madame X, Sargent is more discreet in this area than Milestone. Still,' he added hastily, 'not everyone can afford Sargent and some might see Milestone as reasonable alternative.'

"'To be sure,' I parroted, having not the least idea as to who my informant was talking about.*

"'If I may,' he gestured, and with my acquiescence led me to an adjoining room and pointed. 'These two Sargents are here on consignment. The one to your right is of Lady Brocklehurst and her daughters.† The family have decided to part with it.'

---

*   Possibly as the result of this case, Holmes became more knowledgeable regarding art. By 1916 during the case labeled, *The Telegram from Hell*, the detective could recognize Sargent with ease and compare him with Repin.

†   Madame X, the notorious painting of Sargent's that forced him to leave Paris, depicts Virginie Amélie Gautreau, wife of the French banker Pierre Gautreau. Originally, Sargent painted one strap of her black gown dangling provocatively off her shoulder. This was too much, even for the French, and Sargent repainted it more demurely where it belonged, though the erotic effect of the picture remains much the same. The picture is at New York's Metropolitan Museum of Art. No one has been able to ascertain the present location of Sargent's Lady Brocklehurst.

"What I saw, Watson, truly took my breath away—and, as you know, I do not normally experience difficulty breathing. Amid a background of greenery, I beheld three extraordinary women in white muslin with parasols, posed gracefully under a string of Japanese lanterns within whose rice paper walls gleamed enticing candlelight. I could certainly see the resemblance to Milestone's pictures but fancied I could also detect the difference.

"'And to my left?'

"'Over here,' my guide pointed to the other painting, 'is Dr. Pozzi. It is here on loan only.'

"'Painted in an upstanding rectangle, this image was still more arresting. Dr. Pozzi,* whoever he is, clad in a dressing gown of voluptuous red, offsetting his pale skin, black hair, and beard, stared placidly to one side, the delicate fingers of his right hand splayed over his heart.

"'But my client nonetheless prefers Milestone,' said I, sounding to my own ears, as I did so, a perfect Philistine.

"Brudenell smiled amiably. '*De gustibus non disputandum est.*'†

"'Do you know where I might view or purchase Milestones?'

"'Packwood's,' the man replied without hesitation. 'In Brook Street.'"

"And you followed the trail? Holmes, it's no wonder you're starved."

"Part of detective work is legwork, as you know, Watson. Dreary but occasionally essential. But I had taken the scent and had no

---

*   Sargent's portrait of Dr. Pozzi is currently to be found at the Hammer Museum in Los Angeles.
†   Taste is not a matter for argument.

intention of letting go while it was strong. I made my way to Brook Street and the Packwood gallery where I presented myself as I had done twice before. The place was small and low-ceilinged. One might go so far as to call it intimate, a far cry from the grand establishments I had visited earlier in the day. I was received by a slender young woman who could not have been more than twenty-five. Had she not been taller than usual, I might have described her as having a touch of the gamine." He shook his head as if to clear it. "Her manner was crisp but hospitable. The woman clearly knew what she was about."

It was rare in my experience for Holmes to dwell on the appearance of a woman, unless it bore on one of his investigations.

"And?"

"I asked if Mr. Packwood was in. 'I am Miss Packwood,' she replied in a cheerful Mayfair accent. 'My uncle is usually here in the afternoons.'

"I explained my interest in the paintings of Rupert Milestone. 'I see none on display,' I added, gesturing to the pictures on the walls.

"'We carry some now and again, but Milestone mainly works on commission. We have one or two below and in a day or two I could fetch them up if you'd care to return.'

"'Portraits?' I asked.

"'Seascapes, as I recall.'

"'It's the portraits that interest my client.'

"'Because if it's seascapes, be sure to take a look at that late Turner behind you. Obviously, it's not a Milestone, and in fact fetches rather a good deal more . . .'

"'I'm afraid it's Milestone I'm after,' I said, assuming a crestfallen expression.

"She stood silent for a moment, frowning in thought. 'Then you'd best go to Van Dam's,' said she, brightening.

"'Van Dam's?' I made no attempt to conceal my astonishment.

"She smiled once more. 'They're sure to know. I believe Milestone got his start working at Van Dam's. Sir Johnny is sure to have kept track of him.' She rolled her eyes as she spoke, intimating there was a great deal she might add but evidently decided discretion was preferable to tittle-tattle."

"I knew a Packwood," I interrupted the detective. "'Went up the Khyber Pass with him once upon a time.'"

Holmes leaned forward with interest. "Into Afghanistan? Did you really, Watson? With the Fifth Northumberland?"

"The same." I found myself squaring my shoulders at the memory. "He was a colonel, as I recall. Forgive the interruption. Do I understand you to say Rupert Milestone worked at Van Dam's?'

"The very question I put to Miss Packwood. The question appeared to trouble her.

"'I believe so,' she answered finally.

"'In what capacity?'

"Again, she hesitated. 'As a restorer.'"

"Restorer?" I wasn't sure I'd heard the detective correctly.

Holmes began packing his pipe. I was on the point of remonstrating that the place had just been aired out, but was now so absorbed that I contented myself with my question, which he proceeded to answer. "It's like this, Watson. When you and I visit the National Gallery—"

"When have you last been, Holmes?"

"A figure of speech, my dear fellow. When we visit a museum—*were* we to visit one," he amended, "we look at the pictures and see them pristine in their frames, gleaming with varnish and looking their best. But it turns out that this is seldom the condition in which they were acquired prior to being put on display."

"You don't say."

"When one considers the matter, paintings, like everything else, are inevitably subject to wear and tear—or perhaps I might better say, war and tear. They sit helpless on ancestral walls, pummeled by sunlight, soot, and smoke from nearby hearths, or, stowed in attics, they accumulate layers of dust. Immobile, they are surrounded and menaced by a world replete with battles, flames, pestilence, floods, and bookworms."

"Bookworms?"

"I speak of literal pests like beetles or cockroaches that happily feast on frames, canvas, and paper alike. It requires the services of experts to redress these defects before the results are fit for viewing. Some of their expertise is more involved than others. In simpler cases, the yellowed or cracked varnish must be carefully stripped to reveal the picture's original colours before fresh preservative is applied. In more extreme instances, canvases may have been cut or damaged and some actual painting is required to complete a compromised image. The restorer must be a gifted imitator, able to substitute his craft and possibly his informed imagination for that part of the image that has been lost. Smaller galleries cannot afford the luxury of full-time restorers. In cases such as Packwood's, pictures are restored on an ad hoc basis, but for larger establishments, museums, the National Gallery, and such as Christie's, a restoration department operates more or less full-time."

"And Rupert Milestone—"

"According to my informant, displayed an uncanny aptitude for the practice. He had, in her words, 'technique to burn' and was, in addition, an adroit quick-change artist, capable of adapting his prodigious skill to a variety of differing styles."

As he paused to relight his pipe, I tried to make sense of what I was hearing. "And Mycroft told you Van Dam's is bigger than Christie's and Sotheby's combined—"

"Ergo they are likely obliged to maintain a full-time restoration department." Holmes shook out his match. "But their obligations and difficulties do not end there."

"What do you mean by that?"

"Such institutions must also employ the services of an authenticator."

"An appraiser of sorts?"

"Precisely. One would not wish to spend thousands for a picture whose provenance was uncertain. An authenticator, as I am led to understand, is an expert whose knowledge of the subject and imprimatur lends credibility to the painting's pedigree."

"I was under the impression that only horses, dogs and dukes have pedigrees."

"It turns out pictures and sculptures must possess them as well. Who painted it? Who owned it? Who sold or bequeathed it to whom and so forth. Van Dam's employs the services of a Signor Garibaldi, originally of Florence. Signor Garibaldi's specialty is the Renaissance—in particular, old masters of Italy, France, and the Netherlands."

"Does the authenticator assign a monetary value to the picture?"

"Nothing so cut and dried in the world of art. The picture's worth is determined by market forces. The authenticator merely certifies its legitimacy."

"You appear to have learned a great deal."

"I sense I have merely scratched the surface, so to speak, but needless to say I was intrigued by the data obtained from the captivating Miss Packwood. But I had one final question to pose before wending my way.

"'With the work of restoration requiring such skill, I should imagine restorers make a passable living?' I asked.

"'You must define "passable,"' my informant told me with a smile. 'Mind you, a talent like Milestone's may command somewhat more, but restoration is a feast or famine business, and it is generally known that Lord Southbank squeezes hard. The pay is better than beer money, I daresay, but most restorers are obliged to supplement their incomes by teaching and, inevitably, pursuing their own artistic endeavors.'"

Holmes puffed satisfied smoke. "So there you have it, Watson. However Rupert Milestone makes his agreeable living, restoration work alone does not supply it and neither, it appears, do his pictures, though he achieved some notoriety with his Lady Windermere, which seems to have begat further commissions, at least for a time."

"But the grenadier with whom you spoke at Van Dam's denied any knowledge of Milestone," I remembered.

"Not precisely. You will recall that I have on occasion accused you of observing without seeing—"

"What has seeing to do with this?"

"Only this, that from Doktor Freud we have learned that seeing alone is insufficient. One must also *listen*. Van Dam's greeter specified Van Dam's dealt only in old masters. He said Lord Southbank—or Sir Johnny, if you prefer—did not know of a *painter* by the name Milestone, neatly avoiding naming Milestone as being—or having been—in their employ."

"Why bother?"

"Two reasons occur to me, but there may be others. Primo, he may have wished to spare Milestone's reputation or secondo, and more likely, Van Dam's."

"I don't follow."

"My informant may have wished to avoid acknowledging that Van Dam's employs the services of a restorer. Typically, as I understand, galleries and museums are reluctant to use the word restoration."

I had to laugh. "Too many memories of Charles II?"

Holmes joined in my amusement. "Restoration with a lower-case *r*,"* he said. "Prospective buyers may not be pleased to learn that their purchases may have undergone 'improvements' implied by the term 'restoration.' A tear in the canvas that needs repair they can accept, but they prefer euphemisms like 'conservation' or 'preservation.' After all, what man wishes to pry into the beauty secrets of his mistress?"

---

* Restoration, (capital *R*), refers to the return from exile and *Restoration* of the monarchy under Charles II (the king with those yapping spaniels), following the death of Cromwell.

4

THE ABOMINABLE SNOWMAN

Having eaten and smoked, the detective changed his footwear and left again, returning with a clutch of telegrams in time for supper.

"It is very vexing, Watson," said he, sinking into his deep-cushioned chair, stretching out his long legs, and for once acknowledging his fatigue.

"What is?"

"The whereabouts of Jonathan Van Dam, Sir Johnny, or Lord Southbank, as you please. Cast your eye on this." He leaned forward and handed me one of the telegrams.

I glanced at the brief message:

> LORD SOUTHBANK NOT IN PARIS. STOP. BELIEVE TRAVELED TO NEW YORK FROM SOUTHHAMPTON ABOARD SAXONIA. STOP.

"And this from New York."

"Southbank not in New York," I read aloud. "Believe headed for California. Stop."

"Note the repeated use of the word, 'Believe,'" Holmes sighed. "A most suggestive modifier. One might almost infer no one knows where the great man is."

"And California?"

"It seems Van Dam is something of a European Johnny Appleseed, planting museums rather than apple trees, wherever he sets foot. He established yet another in the village of Pasadena, financed by a railway magnate whose appetite for the finer things bearing his name was whetted by Sir Johnny. 'Peripatetic' fails to do the man justice. It appears Lord Southbank cannot sit still. And there is this from our friends at Scotland Yard."

He handed me yet another telegram:

> PRELIMINARY INQUIRIES DO NOT LOCATE THE NAME MILESTONE AMID SALOPIAN* BIRTH AND DEATH RECORDS. STOP.

I looked up. "So—"

"So Lady Glendenning's notion of Shropshire as the seat of the Milestones would appear to be . . . problematic. Now I come to think of it, I find it would not astonish me to learn that so wonderfully euphonious a name as Rupert Milestone might prove less than original."

---

*   Salopian = a Shropshire native.

With this, the detective heaved himself erect and disappeared into his room.

"Goodnight, Holmes," I called after him. To my surprise he reappeared moments later flourishing a set of latchkeys I knew all too well.

"Nothing of the sort, old man. The snow is melting and my intuition tells me we are approaching a crisis. Could I interest you in a bit of burglary?"

"At number 7, Turncoat Lane?"

"Very good, Watson. Yes, I think we must return to the scene of the crime. Unless I am much mistaken, the police will soon be trampling the evidence. You are aware we are committing a felony?" he added as an afterthought.

"The game's afoot," I responded cheerfully. "And it's not as though we've not ridden to hounds before."

"Capital, my boy! I knew I could depend upon you."

By the time we reached the inconspicuous door of the artist's studio, it was dark. Crowds hurrying home from work, boarding omnibuses, or plunging into the Underground, paid little heed to two gentlemen fumbling for their latchkey.

"Lady Glendenning is not the only possessor of these *passe-partouts*," said Holmes, flourishing a startling assortment. It was only a matter of moments before we found ourselves inside the cavernous space.

"Watson?"

With the door closed and locked behind us, I fetched the two bull's-eyes from the carpet bag and proceeded to light both.

"Where to begin?"

"With the drop cloth, I think," said the detective. "That is surely simplest. Perhaps a closer examination of what the artist was working on at the time of these events will prove instructive."

So saying, we approached the easel and its hidden canvas, which did not appear to have been disturbed from the time we had last visited the place.

"Hold the light a bit higher, doctor."

I did as instructed and the detective carefully removed the cloth, once more exposing the painting. The canvas appeared untouched since our previous visit. Not enclosed by a frame, it was secured with tacks to a board behind it. The result was perplexing.

"Holmes, now that we look more closely, this surely can't have been painted by Rupert Milestone. This looks to be quite old."

"So it does." The detective handed me his lantern to wield in addition to my own. "It is clear that in our haste to examine everything, we did not scrutinize the work as we ought to have done."

He proceeded to pluck a pin from the lapel of his overcoat and searched for an area where the paint seemed thickest. The paint was rock hard, for the pin refused to penetrate the surface at any of a half-dozen points where he attempted it. When at length he broke his silence it was with evident reluctance.

"An uneducated guess—and in my view almost all guesses are uneducated—is that we are looking at a seventeenth-century depiction of Venice, which self-evidently resembles no other city I can think of. There's the Grand Canal with St. Marks in white, there's the Rialto, surely, with several gondolas and barques in the foreground. I have a dim recollection that such as these were painted by men with names like Canaletto or Tintoretto, but I could not swear to either."

"Could it be one of the man's restoration jobs?"

He didn't answer for several moments. "Possibly," he allowed at length. "See the lower right-hand third of the picture."

"Apparently it was never finished," I said, gazing once more at the portion of the painting where the image of Venice faded into blank canvas.

"As you say, Watson, the canvas is clearly old, yet a portion remains unpainted. Bring the lights closer, there's a good fellow."

I obeyed and carried the lights nearer the blank section of the canvas.

"This is surely a restoration project," I repeated. "From what is complete, one could perhaps infer what the painter intended the rest to look like."

Holmes continued to contemplate the picture in silence, bringing his magnifying glass close to the empty portion of the painting. Something like sand crunched beneath his foot and he knelt to inspect it, rubbing his thumb and forefinger with coarse white powder as he rose. "We know too little about this business," he declared at length. "I can imagine a restorer called upon to complete a missing or damaged image, but this—"

Noise from the street below decided him. "Enough. We may be pressing our luck. Let us replace the missing money and look for more before we leave."

With less ceremony than when he removed it, he threw the drop cloth over the incomplete Venetian scene and followed me into the artist's bedroom. With the imposing portrait of the room's occupant seemingly glaring with disapproval at our efforts, I again held my light while the vast sum was stuffed where the detective had found it, inside one of the tasseled brogues. I confess the sight of all that money unguarded and unaccounted for gave me a pang, but Holmes now flourished yet another clutch of banknotes from beneath the mattress.

"As I anticipated, Watson. The man did not put all his eggs in a single basket." Replacing the second fistful of banknotes where he'd found them, the detective got to his feet.

"Perhaps it's time to go," I suggested, for the street noises were making me nervous.

"Faint heart never won fair lady, Watson. Let us first attack the linen chest."

Holmes was obliged to try several keys in his burglar's repertoire before he succeeded in springing the sturdy padlock. As he threw back the lid, I aimed my lantern within the cedar-lined interior to reveal neatly folded sheets and two bulky blankets, one of which boasted several moth holes.

"There doesn't seem to be much of anything—"

"One moment." The detective carelessly heaved the bedding over his shoulder. I heard our joint intake of breath at what we beheld.

"Hullo, what have we here?" The detective held up a diaphanous pink shift.

"That is a peignoir, Holmes."

"You would know, Watson. And this?"

"A camisole."

Holmes continued to extract lace unmentionables. "Interesting," he murmured as he produced, in succession, a scarlet corset, several pairs of dark stockings, and other feminine apparel rightly belonging in a boudoir.

A disquieting notion crossed my mind. "Do you suppose Rupert Milestone to be some kind of—" I hesitated to complete my thought, but Holmes forestalled my question by producing a hairbrush.

"I think not." He held the brush close to his lantern. "Observe the long strands of dark hair caught among the bristles. The hairbrush suggests these items belong to a woman—a woman who spends time here but wishes her presence to remain discreet, hence their place of concealment in a linen chest. And see, here are also less sensational articles of female apparel."

He unwrapped some tissue paper to reveal a toothbrush.

I breathed an inward sigh of relief. "Does that explain the lock, do you think?"

"One moment, old man, there's more to come." Plunging an arm downward, Holmes continued to delve into the recesses of the chest and, with difficulty, managed to extract a lengthy cylinder of stiff cardboard bound with twine, which he held up to his eye as if it were a telescope. "By Jove, there's a painting in here."

"Can you pull it out?"

"And here is another."

A second cylinder was tugged from beneath several pillowcases, the detective taking care not to bend it as he did so. With an effort, he got to his feet. "Returning our plunder under all this bedding if we're obliged to make a hasty exit may prove awkward. Let's wait until we can inspect these curiosities in proper light and at our leisure," he said. "But before we take our leave, let's replace the contents of this chest and lock it as before."

So saying, we spent the next half hour tidying up the place. "What of the picture on the easel?" I asked. "Take it as well?"

Holmes gazed at the drop cloth which covered the unfinished painting, stroking his lips with the tips of his fingers. "I expect its absence would be too quickly noticed," he said finally. "I will take the carpet bag if you can manage these, old man? Mind you don't crease them." So saying, he handed me the two cylinders. Gingerly, I managed to cache the two coiled paintings under my coat. Neither was heavy and without further ado, we made our way out of the place, by which time the streets were largely deserted.

The trains were no longer running and we were compelled to walk several blocks in a pattering rain before managing to flag a hansom. The cabbie was on the point of quitting for the evening and required persuading to take another fare. It was after midnight when we reached Baker Street and the door was bolted, obliging us to rouse the long-suffering Mrs. Hudson, who admitted us without comment, accustomed by now to the odd hours kept by the lodgers at 221B.

"Holmes, I confess I am on fire to see what is in those cylinders."

By way of reply the detective yawned and leaned back in his seat. "As am I," he returned, "though I suspect I will be sharper after a good night's sleep. I've been on the go for upwards of forty hours and will do better when I am fresh."

I was disappointed by this, but in any event, it was not to be. It felt as though I had only slept ten minutes when I was awakened by a sharp knocking.

"Mr. Holmes! Dr. Watson," I could hear Mrs. Hudson's muffled voice on the other side of our door, "the police are here!"

Fumbling for my robe, I opened the door to find our faithful housekeeper in nightwear and slippers, hair unpinned, overshadowed two hulking constables.

"Mr. 'olmes?" One man touched two fingers to his helmet.

"Mr. Holmes is asleep. I am—"

"I'm right here, Watson," said the detective behind me, tying the sash on his mouse-coloured dressing gown. "Gentlemen, I am Sherlock Holmes. What has happened?"

"Beg pardon for the disturbance, Mr. 'olmes," the policeman again deferentially touched the brim of his helmet, "but Inspector Gregson sends his compliments and begs you to join him in Kensington Gardens."

"Kensington Gardens?" I wasn't sure I'd heard the man correctly and I could see Holmes shared my confusion.

"Just opposite the palace, sir. And 'e says to tell you 'e's sent for Lady Glendenning."

"Lady Glendenning?" It seemed all I could manage was to echo every sentence.

"Well, sir, seems as it was Lady Glendenning what first filed the missing person's report."

"Quick, Watson, into your clothes and fetch your bag," Holmes touched my shoulder. "The crisis seems to have arrived even sooner than expected."

Somewhat incongruously, we were bundled into a waiting Black Maria and trotted briskly off, bound, presumably, for Kensington Palace, though the barred windows of our transport did not allow us to see much.

"Holmes, what do you think has happened?"

The detective, his expression dimly lit within the confines of the wagon, favored me with a solemn look.

"I think the snow has melted faster than I anticipated, Watson."

Neither of us could think of anything further to say. All was silent save the muffled hoofbeats of the horses and the occasional sounds that hinted at places we passed. Eventually, we drew to a halt and the barred door was opened.

"We're 'ere, gents."

Kensington Gardens remained blanketed by a thin layer of snow. Without their mantle of green, the branches of the majestic chestnut trees appeared forlorn and lachrymose with melting ice. But the sight which greeted us when we stepped down and into the light was unfamiliar to me. A police cordon consisting of tarpaulins masking a large circle had been erected, effectively hiding what lay within the perimeter of the playground.

By now, the place teemed with curious onlookers, many of whom were nannies escorting small children, come to play in the welcome sunshine.

"Mind how you go. Keep the kiddies clear and stand back, if you please," were the repeated instructions delivered, I thought, in a deliberately casual monotone.

"Mr. Holmes."

"Inspector Gregson. What have we here?"

"A bad business, sir." The white-faced man frowned. "If you'll follow me."

Gregson looked much the same, though his once dark hair was now flecked with gray. On previous occasions, genial banter between the detective and the policeman was not uncommon. Holmes and Gregson were accustomed to ribbing one another, each calling into question his rival's methods and abilities. But no such levity was occurring here.

"And Lady Glendenning?"

"Lestrade 'as notified her, though I'm not sure that was the wisest course, but then you know Lestrade, always rushing in where angels . . ."

His voice trailed off as Holmes and I brushed past him through a gap in the hastily staked tarpaulins.

I can scarcely trust myself to describe what I saw, though I know the sight will remain forever burned on my brain. A snowman was melting, revealing, as it did so, portions of a clothed, frozen body within it—a face, an arm, part of a leg. Seldom had I ever viewed anything that so repulsed me. Even Sherlock Holmes hesitated briefly before nerving himself to examine it.

"Ingenious," he declared quietly. "Now we know where and how the murderer managed to conceal his victim. Given our succession of winter blizzards, it had occurred to me a snowbank might have been a possible repository, postponing the moment of discovery and allowing the killer time for his escape, but I confess I did not foresee a snowman."

"It might have stayed hidden still longer had the children not begun pelting it with snowballs," Gregson said, drawing up behind us.

What we saw was a man of middle age with curled, once-yellow hair, now darkened by melting ice so that only golden glints peeped through. Water oozed down the clean-shaven face, causing the handsome features to sag, dripping from the artist's once pugnacious chin. The frigid eyes were rheumy, as if the deceased suffered from cataracts. The effect curiously put me in mind of a wax effigy I had once seen being softened for repair at Madame Tussaud's.

"Holmes, this is beyond my experience, but the body has been more or less preserved by the temperature."

"That is doubtless why there is no odor of putrefaction as yet." Holmes inspected the dead man closely, talking to me over his shoulder as he did so. "The clothes appear a tight fit."

"Because the corpse bloated before it froze. The clothing will loosen as it thaws."

He nodded. "The cause of death, I take it, is the slashed throat of the victim?"

"Beyond question. Though all blood has long since departed the body, there is a gash where the throat was cut."

Holmes took a step back. "The man appears to have been well-dressed at the time of the altercation that led to his death."

It was not difficult to confirm the detective's observation. Brown stains had ruined the Turnbull & Asser shirt, but the effusion that followed had miraculously missed the artist's waistcoat and Prince Albert cutaway. "Doubtless pitching forward as he died, the rest of his clothing escaped bloodstains," I noted.

The detective found a twig and used it to prize open the victim's frozen broadcloth coat. "Huntsman and Sons, Savile Row," he murmured, squinting at the label. "'Tailored for Rupert Milestone.'"

The detective produced his magnifying glass and was now peering through it at the corpse's pale fingers. "This is curious," he murmured when a tremulous cry interrupted his examination.

"Ah, no! Great heavens, no!" Behind us, Lady Glendenning broke from clasping Inspector Lestrade's arm and staggered toward the grotesque figure, which all the while dripped water from its rapidly dissolving carapace. Her stumbling steps caused some of her ash-white hair to come unpinned, but she paid no heed.

Had Holmes not restrained her, Lady Glendenning appeared ready to trip headlong into the dead man.

"Your ladyship," Gregson spoke quietly behind her, "do you know this man?"

Held upright between us, Lady Glendenning drew several sharp breaths as she endeavored to collect herself, finally managing to state in a choked voice, "That is my tenant, Rupert Milestone."

"You are certain?"

The reply was a curt nod. The truant strands of hair were pushed absently back into place.

Two coroner's orderlies now arrived and we led the stricken woman aside, still supporting her against the possibility of collapse, as the men engaged in the difficult task of tipping the body onto a stretcher. Their efforts at decorum were frustrated by the posture of the dead man. After a hasty exchange, it was judged preferable not to spend time attempting to free the corpse from its frozen location. The decision made it appear a snowman was being rushed to the mortuary.

Gregson acknowledged the newly arrived Lestrade with a grimace and proceeded to ignore him, addressing a nearby constable holding a notebook at the ready. "Let the record show the witness has identified the body as belonging to that of—" He turned to face our client.

"Rupert Milestone," Lady Glendenning repeated in a hoarse voice. Then, as if startled to find herself propped between Holmes and myself, she added, "I take it the case of my missing rent money is now at an end."

With the removal of the corpse (under cover of a sheet and looking for all the world like a civic monument yet to be unveiled), the police cordon was rapidly disassembled, allowing the gawkers a clear view of nothing in particular. Children and nannies wandered eagerly into the empty playground and in no time joyous shouting had resumed and the entire scene had returned to normal.

5

THE SECOND LADY GLENDENNING

"I cannot thank you gentlemen enough," said Lady Glendenning, seated at her writing table, signing, then handing over a generous cheque to the detective.

We were in the study of Lord Glendenning's resplendent home in Grosvenor Square where tea had been laid on. A sudden jingling bell startled the detective and myself.

"Pay no attention," said Lady Glendenning. "It's the telephone I made the mistake of installing. The wretched thing shrieks at all hours and I can never make out a word on the other end."

She picked up the earpiece, cutting off the bell, before setting it down again. "That's better. What was I saying? Oh, thanking you for your help."

"It seems to me we have done very little," responded Holmes, folding and pocketing the cheque. "Inspector Gregson handled matters from the time the snowman was discovered. But the fact remains, your tenant's murderer is still at large and thus the situation must be accounted . . . fluid."

Lady Glendenning took a deep breath in response to these tidings. "I understand," she said soberly, "but what am I to do?" She threw out her hands in a helpless gesture. "This business has upset me terribly. I must try to recover from the shock and continue to oversee my husband's affairs. Until I wed Lord Glendenning I very much had to make my own way in the world. Basil then saw to my every need, but now he is gone, I am burdened with a great many additional and pressing responsibilities. I must remember that Rupert Milestone's problems were not mine. It is the concern of the police to apprehend the fiend who did this, wouldn't you agree, Mr. Holmes? Mr. Holmes?"

"I beg your pardon," Holmes turned to face her. "I was admiring this framed theatrical program. You were an actress?"

Lady Glendenning smiled, faintly embarrassed. "Not really, but that is how I chanced to meet my husband. Lord Glendenning had it framed for what one would term sentimental reasons."

"Oh?"

In the manner of other couples recounting the days of their courtship, the memory pleased and diverted her. "As a young woman, merely to amuse myself after work, you understand—I was a typist—I joined a neighborhood amateur theatrical troupe, The Putney Players."

"And—?"

"And Basil—Lord Glendenning—chanced to be in the vicinity on business when he was caught in a downpour. It was raining cats and dogs and the poor man dodged into the theatre with little thought of the fate that awaited him. We were playing *Candida* at the time."

"Bernard Shaw?" Holmes refrained from claiming acquaintance with the playwright.[*]

Her smile broadened. "Yes, I was Candida, rather too young for the part but with amateur theatricals, last-minute compromise is often the order of the day. In any event, it was love across the footlights. And you may imagine our amusement when we realized my admirer was my landlord!"

"A romantic story," I said, setting down my teacup.

She laughed. "It is, rather. Basil loved to tell it and of course he had the program framed to commemorate our encounter, but in truth, the likes of Mrs. Patrick Campbell had little to fear from me. I was a most indifferent actress. After meeting Basil, I shortly thereafter retired from the stage. The stage's loss was Lord Glendenning's gain. And mine." She smiled sadly now.

"Lady Glendenning, we've taken up enough for your time. The sooner we depart, the sooner you can begin the business of recovering from this grotesque experience."

"That is my hope. Thank you again, Mr. Holmes."

As we left, we could make out the infernal machine clanging once more and the exasperated moan of its owner. "Hello? Hello?? Who is speaking?"

---

[*] Shaw was a former client of Holmes's, as recounted in *The West End Horror.*

"I suppose one day I must succumb," Holmes remarked sourly as we stood on the curb outside the large house in search of a cab.

"Succumb?"

"To the telephone. It's the triumph of utility over serenity. Driver!"

"Lady Glendenning may imagine the case is over," Holmes said later, endorsing Lady Glendenning's cheque after our return to Baker Street, "but that hardly explains how Rupert Milestone ended up a snowman in Kensington Gardens. Granted, the park is conveniently close to Notting Hill, so the body had not far to travel, but there are several features of this business which remain unreconciled as far as this office is concerned."

"I'm sure Scotland Yard agrees," I said. "Who killed the man, for a start."

"And with what weapon, Watson."

I frowned. "The razor that has gone missing from Milestone's bathroom, surely," I answered. "Doubtless that was easier to get rid of than the body."

"Doubtless. But how did the razor make the trek from Milestone's wash basin, where, based on the hairs still there, it had been recently used for shaving, to the place where the two men struggled near the easel? I think we have established that the killing was spontaneous but are we to believe that as heated words became blows, the killer broke off hostilities long enough to visit the bathroom and return with the murder weapon?"

"I see your point. Even assuming such a chain of events plausible, are we to assume the painter waited patiently for his murderer to rummage for it in the next room?"

"Precisely." The detective closed his eyes but I knew he was far from sleep. He resumed speaking with his eyes shut. "And curious so little blood was spilled on the victim's frock coat."

"It was certainly on his shirt. But as I noted, in death the man may have bent so far forward—"

"So you did." He opened his eyes. "Do you remember the Venetian cityscape we left behind in our recent flight from Milestone's studio?"

"Of course."

"Do you remember that a substantial portion of the canvas was bare, suggesting the painting was unfinished or incomplete?"

"Holmes, it was only yesterday. Of course I remember. What are you getting at?"

"Only this. Among the tidbits I gleaned from my recent cram course in art is the fact that paint is never applied directly to a naked canvas."

"I'm not sure I follow."

"The canvas must be prepared before the artist wields his brush. A mixture of white paint and eggs the Italians term *gesso* is applied before actual painting can begin. The intention is to create a poreless surface so the colours are not diluted by absorption into the canvas."

"I'm afraid I still don't understand."

The detective closed his eyes again, remembering.

"The empty portion of the Venetian scene on Rupert Milestone's easel was devoid of gesso. It was untreated, bare canvas, no sealant in evidence. But there is absolutely no question in my mind that were we able to see or search beneath the painting that remains, we would most certainly encounter gesso. Which, viewing the blank portion of the canvas, we did not."

"What does that tell you?"

He sighed and opened his eyes. "I wish I knew. I only know that what I saw from a painter's standpoint was irregular and it is irregularities that suggest significance, the exception that probes the rule."

"I think you mean 'proves the rule,' Holmes."

My companion frowned with a trace of irritation. "I tend to mean what I say, Watson. If one considers the matter at all, how can an exception to a rule prove anything, except, possibly, that the rule is wrong? It is that common confusion of *p*s and *b*s that bequeaths us that nonsensical adage. The exception is what *tests* the rule, hence the word probe is correct." He stifled a yawn. "I think perhaps the time has come to examine our spoils of war."

"I beg your pardon?"

He smiled. "Surely you've not forgot the two canvases we brought back last night?"

"By Jove, in light of what just transpired, I confess they completely slipped my mind. I don't imagine I will ever forget the sight of that snowman."

"Nor will I," said the detective. "Did you notice the curious detail of the corpse's fingernails?"

"The fingernails appeared pristine to me."

"That is the curious detail."

"Holmes, in heaven's name open the cylinders!"

"Very well." But he remained in contemplative silence several moments longer before energetically turning to the task at hand.

Using his penknife to sever the twine, he tugged gently at the canvas within the first cylinder, pulling it forth, unfurling and spreading it on the rug as I peered over his shoulder.

"Great Scott!"

Rocking back on his heels, Holmes reached up for an ashtray to pin one corner of the image, gesturing to me to hand him a paperweight to secure another, and using the corner of a footrest to secure a third.

"Holmes, this is obscene."

Holmes gazed impassively at the image. "Obscene perhaps, but not uncommon. Representations of unclothed men and women constitute a significant portion of artistic subject matter, dating back centuries. Even you and I know as much. Greeks and Romans sculpted the human figure and painters have found a ready market for nakedness ever since. The line between obscenity and art, one suspects, is fodder for endless debate."

"Holmes, I know obscenity when I see it."

The detective appeared in no hurry to accept my argument. "Is it the fact that the picture is clearly modern rather than ancient that offends you? If it were a marble statue missing one of its arms, or perhaps a head, would you be more at ease with it? This image may be off the beaten track, I grant you, but in another hundred years, who is to say? One age's obscenity may be another's masterpiece. Painters, sculptors, composers, and writers are frequently ahead of the mass of humanity. I suspect the same is true of fashion. What did people make of Beau Brummell's latest ensemble before every gentleman was ordering his tailor to emulate it? Beauty or obscenity—all dwell in the eye of the beholder. On occasion, I would wager, simultaneously."

He dragged the leg of the nearest chair to hold down the last corner of the picture before standing next to me. The unpainted white border of the canvas was punctured with nail holes from the time it had been stretched on a frame.

I was forced to entertain a portion of the detective's argument. What we saw, though risqué, was also, I had to admit, exquisite. A pale, nude woman, clad only in a slender black ribbon around her throat and a pink flower behind one ear, reclined on a white divan and stared brazenly at the viewer with bright blue eyes. Behind her, a turbaned Negress stood in attendance, holding what looked like a bouquet, doubtless sent by an admirer.

Holmes moved to the door, opened it, and called down. "Mrs. Hudson, have you such a thing as a hatpin? No, you needn't come in, thank you so much."

Hatpin in hand, he closed the door on the inquisitive woman and knelt once more beside the picture. "As I thought," he said, holding up the pin with its dab of white paint. "This is fresh."

"Why shouldn't it be?" I spluttered. "This is Milestone's work, doubtless on a par with his Lady Windermere that caused such an uproar. The subject is obviously the woman whose undergarments were cached in the linen chest. The hair colour matches the strands on the hairbrush."

"Indubitably. Very good, my boy. Leaving only the question of for whom this was painted."

"Considering it could hardly be displayed."

"Ah, you never know, Watson. A tribute from the painter to his coy mistress, perhaps. Something for only them to enjoy. Shall we have a look at the other canvas?"

Without waiting for my reply, he sliced the twine around the second cylinder and, seeking more space, rearranged the clutter on the table containing his chemical apparatus, securing the corners of the picture with a Bunsen burner and his microscope.

I had no idea what to expect—another prurient image?—but what we beheld was, in its way, more shocking than the first.

"Holmes, this is a Rembrandt!"

"A self-portrait. Yes, Watson. Just as many who have never seen the play know what a Romeo is, even such ignoramuses as we can recognize a Rembrandt when we see one." He looked over his shoulder. "What have I done with Mrs. H's hatpin? Never mind—" He pulled open one of the table's drawers and, after fishing for it, produced a familiar case of worn Moroccan leather.

"Holmes, are you certain this is—"

"Not to worry, old man." So saying, with thin, nervous fingers the detective snapped open the lid and held up the hypodermic that recalled such harrowing memories. "I expect this will do."

As I watched, Holmes attempted to insert the needle into various parts of Rembrandt's face, clothing, and shadowy background—all without success.

"Hard as agate," he observed, setting down the syringe, its tip now blunted and shaft bent beyond further use. "It appears we are confronted by a Rembrandt self-portrait. What can it be doing in the late Rupert Milestone's linen chest?"

"Holmes, the fact that the paint is hard suggests only its age, not its authorship. Neither of us is qualified to determine what we are looking at."

Holmes broke off his contemplation of the picture to smile at me.

"Invaluable, Watson!"

"How so?"

He was searching for his coat. "Because you have opened up our next level of inquiry. I think we must pay a call on Signor Garibaldi."

"Who?"

"Van Dam's authenticator."

6

RIGOLETTO

Once more at Van Dam's, the grenadier, as Holmes had dubbed him, made little attempt to conceal his pique at the sight of the American from Kansas. The nameplate on the counter identified him as Mr. Foggerty.

"Ah, Mr.—"

"Gilmore," Holmes reminded him in a drawl, offering a smile that threatened to topple into a grin. "Jasper Gilmore, turning up again like the bad penny."

"Mr. Gilmore, as I've endeavored to explain," Mr. Foggerty began with frosty impatience, "Lord Southbank is out of town and—"

"Oh, let's forget about all that," Holmes breezily cut him off. "Me and Mr. Jones here"—gesturing in my direction—"have come on another matter entirely."

"Oh?" He raised a skeptical eyebrow.

"Yessir, Mr. Jones here thinks he's found a Rembrandt."

On cue, I handed over the cylinder, again secured with a stretch of twine.

It was all Foggerty could manage to contain his amusement. "Is that so? Unfortunately, I'm rather pressed for—"

"Totally understand," Holmes again cut off the gatekeeper. "This won't take but a moment. Is there someplace we can—"

Mr. Foggerty relished the opportunity of interrupting the insolent American in turn. "I'm sure that won't be necessary," he fairly smirked. "Let's have a look right here, why don't we?"

"As you please," said Jasper Gilmore. Suiting action to the word, Holmes snipped the twine, gently unrolled the canvas, and slid the painting across the counter to the factotum.

The effect produced at the sight of the picture was remarkable. The monocle dropped from its lodging and the man's eyes seemed on the point of popping from their sockets. Instinctively, his hands pinned the edges of the canvas as if to prevent the image slipping from his grasp.

"Where did you come by this?" Foggerty's tone of harried condescension was now replaced by an awed whisper. He tore his gaze from the picture long enough to throw a furtive look over his shoulder at the busy gallery before returning to scrutinize the portrait that dazzled him.

"Now let's not get carried away," said Jasper Gilmore. "The first thing we need to know is if this thing's for real."

Instead of answering, Foggerty, whose ramrod posture had now declined to a stoop (putting me in mind of a balloon leaking air), seemed unable to wrest his gaze from the painting. With fingers that convulsively clenched and unclenched, he spun the canvas this way and that on the counter, bringing his head up close to the brushwork before jerking it back.

"Well, can you let us know?" Holmes clearly enjoyed tormenting the haughty representative. It struck me the detective was pushing his luck. I seldom saw Holmes overact, but he was in danger of losing himself in the role.

"It is not for me to say," Foggerty said at length, still peering intently at the image and touching the paint with tremulous fingers. It was as if he feared to blink for fear the vision would disappear.

"Yup, I figured as much. Too much responsibility, I shouldn't wonder. Don't worry, I won't hold you to it," Holmes said. He tugged the picture from under Foggerty's hands and rolled it casually up again, as if it were no more than a sheepskin diploma, causing the man to gasp. "We're thinking we need to talk to Signor Garibaldi."

Once again, Van Dam's greeter was taken by surprise. "Signor Garibaldi?"

"Your authenticator. Signor Garibaldi is said to be the best." Holmes looked around. "Is he on the premises?"

"He is not." Foggerty responded automatically. "Signor Garibaldi works from his home."

"In Italy?" I felt it incumbent upon myself to prove I was not mute.

Foggerty made no attempt to conceal his annoyance. "No."

"He's in town then?" asked Holmes. "Kindly let us have his address we'll trot 'round to—"

Like a balloon replenished with air, Foggerty's ramrod posture returned, the monocle once more secure in its niche. "Due to the sensitive nature of their work, Van Dam's does not divulge the addresses of its employees. If you'd care to leave the picture here, I'm sure—"

"I think not," said Holmes briskly. "Please tell Lord Southbank we stopped by."

Foggerty did his best to appear unfazed by this latest turn of events, though he was unable entirely to conceal his disappointment.

"Good day, gentlemen."

In short order we found ourselves outside the grandiose monstrosity.

"Now what?" I demanded. "Are we to hang about until we catch sight of Signor Garibaldi and trail him to his place of business with our questions?"

The detective frowned. "As we've no description of the man, nor any idea when and how often he puts in an appearance here, that approach may prove problematic." Just as quickly, his countenance cleared. "But we needn't be downcast, Watson. I am certain we can come up with something more efficient. Come, let us set about it."

Some hours later, I woke from an afternoon nap to find Holmes in conversation with a slender youth I knew I had seen before. The detective was wrapping a parcel in brown paper.

"Watson, you remember Wiggins," he said.

"Wiggins! By Jove, I knew I recognized you! How you've grown!"

"Thankee, doctor." Now at least eighteen, the young man's voice had dropped but its owner was indeed the former leader of the group of street Arabs the detective employed on occasion to ferret out secrets or trail suspects where a uniform would have brought unwanted attention. Holmes dubbed these urchins The Baker

Street Irregulars, rewarding them a shilling each for their services. There was no telling what had become of that posse of ragamuffins by now but Wiggins had clearly managed to better himself.

"I work at Lidgates,* doctor," he explained, anticipating my question.

"Bravo," I responded as Holmes concluded tying off the parcel.

"Wiggins, as you may see, this parcel is addressed to a Signor Garibaldi at Van Dam's in Piccadilly. But before you attempt to deliver it, you are to drop in at the Savoy Theatre in the Strand and ask for Richard D'Oyly Carte, who owes me a favor he will not hesitate to grant."†

"D'Oyly Carte at the Savoy," the youth repeated.

Sherlock Holmes handed him a scribbled note. "At my request, he will take you to the theatre costume shop where you will be kitted out as a youthful commissionaire."

"I see."

"In that guise you will approach Mr. Foggerty at Van Dam's in Piccadilly, explaining your parcel is for Signor Garibaldi *from Mr. Milestone in Notting Hill.*"

"Mr. Milestone in Notting Hill," Wiggins dutifully echoed.

"Mr. Foggerty will then explain Signor Garibaldi is not on the premises and offer to deliver your parcel to him, but under no circumstances are you to agree to this. I repeat: you are not to let the parcel out of your hands. You will explain you have been

---

* The butcher shop—still in business.
† In the wake of a murder at the Savoy, Holmes was of assistance to impresario Richard D'Oyly Carte, chronicled by Watson in the case known as *The West End Horror*.

explicitly instructed by Mr. Milestone to deliver it into no hands other than Signor Garibaldi's. If he is not on the premises, you are to insist on Signor Garibaldi's address, as the matter is most urgent. Mr. Foggerty will reluctantly find himself obliged to provide this to you."

"And then?"

"You will telegraph the address to me."

"After I deliver the parcel?"

"You are to do nothing of the kind," said Holmes sternly.

The youth frowned. "Nothing of the—then where should I—?"

"It is a matter of complete indifference to me, Wiggins, as the contents are entirely worthless—unless you are keen to read back numbers of the *Pall Mall Gazette*."

The young man now smiled in turn. "Hee-hee. Very clever, Mister 'olmes."

"Let us hope so," the detective said. "There's a guinea in it for you if all goes according to plan."

"That's a big improvement over the shilling," Wiggins laughed and there I suddenly beheld the impish grin I remembered from the boy's rapscallion days.

"And now we wait," I suggested after Wiggins had closed the door behind him.

"Tedious but necessary. Another part of the detective's drudgery, as you well know, Watson."

It was midafternoon when the telegram was delivered.

"Number 12 Cheyne Walk, Chelsea. Stop," Holmes read aloud. He looked up, making a failed attempt not to appear smug. "We must be sure Wiggins receives his guinea at Lidgates."

"I believe Sir Thomas More lived nearby," Holmes remarked as he pulled the bell next to the red painted door of number 12. It was almost four and behind the detective, late afternoon river traffic on the Thames hooted and whistled beneath the Prince Albert Bridge, almost entirely blocking our view of the unsightly warehouses in Battersea. "It's difficult to imagine this part of London was tranquil countryside when Henry VIII visited Sir Thomas and his family here."

The house with its small mullioned windows was one of several ancient structures, dating, as Holmes suggested, more or less to the time of the martyred Lord High Chancellor.

"Do you think Foggerty has notified Signor Garibaldi of our intention to pay a call?"

"I should be astonished to learn he did not at least make the attempt." Holmes tugged more vigorously this time. We could hear the bell clang within.

The door was opened by a maid. *"Sì?"* Dressed in black, she was middle-aged and stout, her jet black hair streaked with white on one side.

"Jasper Gilmore to see Signor Garibaldi." Holmes produced another of his cards.

The woman stared at it, regarding us and our parcel with a foreigner's suspicion. *"Aspetta."* Without ceremony, she slammed the door in our faces and we could make out the bolt shooting with finality.

"She is illiterate," Holmes commented. "To her way of thinking, it is we who are the suspicious foreigners."

After several moments, even with that heavy obstacle between us, we could make out excited Italian voices, a man's growls furiously overriding the woman's soprano. Shortly thereafter, the bolt slid back and the door was reopened.

"*Venite, per favore.*" Head bowed low, the chastened servant stood aside to admit us. "*Signor Garibaldi!*" she trilled. This was followed by a flood of rapid-fire Italian, presumably announcing our approach.

The narrow house in which we found ourselves bore scant resemblance to a modern English home. Electricity had not yet been installed and, though gaslit, darkness prevailed, as must have been the case since the place's earliest days. Nonetheless the Italians, famed for their taste, had contrived to make their mark here and the result more closely resembled a Tuscan villa (as I imagined one) than a residence on the Embankment. Sounds of the river could scarcely be made out behind thick walls and the heavy door, and it took some effort to remember we were not forty paces from the Thames. As suits of armour have proved, men were smaller in that bygone time, and Holmes, above six feet, was obliged to dodge lintels as we made our way down a slender corridor, the walls of which were festooned with paintings in gilt frames. A creaking floor overlaid with a tufted runner softened our footsteps.

"It is very dark, Holmes."

"I have learned paintings do not do well when overexposed to sunlight," the detective murmured. "Like the late Rupert Milestone, one may surmise our authenticator lives well," he added.

At the other end of the dim passageway, a light beckoned, drawing us toward what proved an intimate chamber. From the objects in view, I understood we were entering the authenticator's workroom.

"*Venite!*" boomed the male voice we had heard before. "*Grazie, Leopoldina.*"

Signor Garibaldi was seated in the low-ceilinged room, behind which a modern conservatory enclosed what had once been a small back garden. The second most arresting feature in the place was a mirror affixed to the low ceiling, positioned directly above a long worktable. At the farther end, deposited in empty paint and tobacco cannisters, I beheld rulers, pincers, brushes, tweezers, calipers, and various instruments whose names and function were unknown to me.

But the room's chief surprise was its sole occupant. Signor Garibaldi was a hunchback. Clothed in a red quilted smoking jacket whose design took into consideration its owner's shape, and glaring at us from his vantage point in a specially constructed, high-backed chair, was Van Dam's authenticator. The slender hand he held up as we entered was holding the earpiece of a telephone, while the other clutched the rest of the instrument as he shouted into it.

"*Bene! Bene! Sì!* I will attend to it." The speaker's English was heavily accented. "Tell his lordship! *Arrivederci.*" Awkwardly he jammed the earpiece into its cradle and set down the contraption, making no attempt to rise.

"*Signori.*" No longer shouting, his sonorous voice sounded as though it came equipped with its own echo. "To why do I owe the pleasure?" Though the pronunciation was foreign, the voice itself was as enveloping as velvet.

"We were directed to consult with you by Mr. Foggerty at Van Dam's," Holmes explained, still in character as the American from Kansas, "regarding the authenticity of this painting."

The man regarded us in silence.

"Will you take a look?" Holmes asked, undismayed.

Another hesitation was followed by a stern reply. *"Indicate."* A jeweled forefinger imperiously jutted downward at the bare table.

Holmes nodded in my direction and I slid the canvas from its cylinder, placing it below the gaze of the expert, comprehending, as I did so, the purpose of the overhead mirror, for it provided an unimpeded view of anything beneath it. As Signor Garibaldi craned forward to peer upward into the mirror, I had the opportunity to study the man. Despite his misshapen form and disproportionately massive head, his features, like his voice, were not displeasing. One might even have called Garibaldi handsome were it not for his impairment. His broad brow was pale in contrast to his ruddy cheeks and ebony beard. Coupled with his red smoking jacket, he briefly put me in mind of the Sargent portrait Holmes had described to me of Dr. Pozzi.

If the sight of a putative Rembrandt elicited any response from the authenticator, I could hardly detect it. Only the slightest twitch at the sight betrayed his response.

Garibaldi now held the picture up by its corners, enabling him to examine the canvas from its obverse. "Seventeen century. Dutch. The verso look right," he murmured at length.

"Verso?"

"Back."

Holmes said nothing to this.

"But no has varnish," Signor Garibaldi commented, as transfixed by the image as Foggerty had been. The word *varnish* revealed the man's curiously predatory teeth.

"What does that tell you?" Holmes asked.

There was an imperceptible shrug. Garibaldi placed another finger gently on Rembrandt's chin, then, taking up a magnifying glass he scowled through it, murmuring to himself, not unlike the detective when examining evidence at the scene of a crime.

"*Ecco.*" Another shrug of the mismatched shoulders as a fingernail scratched the surface. "Varnish remov-ed. Or possibly is no applied."

"Why would someone remove the varnish?"

Signor Garibaldi finally deigned to look from the picture to Holmes.

"Because of *craquelure*."

"Because of what?"

"Craquelure," he repeated slowly. "Varnish make yellow over time and crack appear across surface, like parch-ed desert, *capite*? This is not uncommon. Surely you have seen. *Ecco*, varnish must be stripped and replac-ed."

"In other words, an act of restoration?"

"*Forse.* Perhaps," he translated for our benefit.

"Is that your opinion, Signor Garibaldi?"

The authenticator returned to his perusal of the picture as if he had not heard. "*Brilliante*," he whispered.

"We know it's brilliant. But is it real?" I demanded. "Is it a Rembrandt?"

He turned to look at me as if I, not he nor the canvas, were the curiosity in the room. "Signor, I am paid to determine such things."

"How much?" inquired the detective. This produced a harsh peal of laughter.

"If you must ask, you cannot afford! After all," this was followed by another guttural laugh, "I must have some compensation for this," and he jerked two forefingers over his shoulders in the general vicinity of his crooked spine.

"May I ask, how long you have been employed by Lord Southbank?" Holmes said.

Garibaldi stared but made no answer.

"Are you on retainer or are you paid by the job? Do you receive a commission on pictures you authenticate?"

"Who are you?" The voice was no longer a reassuring velvet. The predatory teeth flashed.

"That is the question I am putting to you," said Sherlock Holmes.

A staring contest between the two men ensued. Feeling there was little more to be gained at this juncture and worried much might be lost, I began to reroll the picture, when a hand was gently laid over mine. I was startled as much by the touch of cool flesh as by the sight of the slender and graceful hand itself, so at odds with the rest of its owner.

"May I keep for further study? A day or two only. *Prometto*."

"Why?" the detective demanded bluntly.

The authenticator resumed staring at Holmes. "*Curiosità*."

Holmes appeared to entertain the possibility, but just as abruptly changed his mind. "So sorry," he said briskly. "Come along,

Hamish, we've taken up enough of the authenticator's time. Good day, Signor Garibaldi."

"Who are you?" repeated the authenticator.

The detective reached into his waistcoat and from its leather case produced a different card.

"*Mi chiamo* Sherlock Holmes," he said, setting it on the table between them.

The Italian, already pale, picked up the card, scanned its contents, and turned ashen. "*Uscite!*"

"I take it this is an invitation to leave," said Holmes, bowing slightly in the direction of the speaker.

The hunchback regarded us wordlessly, his fierce, glinting eyes bent upon us as we made our way back through the darkened hallway. Outside the entrance of number 12, Holmes bent over, giving way to one of his silent fits of laughter.

"Was it wise to reveal your identity?"

"I could not resist, Watson. You know of my fondness for the dramatic."

"Do you think Foggerty warned him of our coming?"

He shook his head, wiping tears of mirth with the back of his hand. "Possibly. You will recall my telling you of Mycroft's injunction: art dealers are not fond of questions pertaining to anything but pictures and profit. Other inquiries, as we have lately observed, are decidedly unwelcome. But even had Foggerty warned him, Signor Garibaldi's choices were limited. Whether he knew we were coming or not, short of barring the door or attempting to convince us he was not at home, what could the poor man do but examine the painting? All he managed was to avoid taking a position as to its authenticity."

"Why would he wish to do that?" I asked.

"Why indeed, Watson? What had Signor Garibaldi—or gatekeeper Foggerty, for that matter—have to lose by venturing an opinion regarding the picture? The best the authenticator could manage was that the varnish had been removed, or not yet applied, which even a layman might discern. And so we have two mysterious paintings, one missing its undercoat of gesso and another its overcoating of varnish. As to the age of the canvas—"

"Holmes!" I flung myself at the detective as a hansom bore down at a furious gallop, thrusting him out of its path in time to save his neck and tumbling us both to the cobblestones as the horse, never breaking stride, clattered out of sight. All I managed to see before they rounded the corner on one wheel, was the cabbie, scarf flying, cracking his whip smartly above the animal's head. "Are you all right?"

"Let me out from under and we shall see."

With difficulty, I managed to heave my bulk off the detective as we struggled to our feet. Holmes was covered with black slush but appeared otherwise unharmed.

"It appears I owe you my life, or something very like it, Watson," he said, smearing his forehead with the back of a snow-stained sleeve.

I affected to ignore this comment though in fact it meant a great deal to me. I could not offhand count the number of times the detective had saved my skin. "Fellow never even stopped," I responded, brushing myself off in turn. "Cabbies drive like madmen these days."

"Some do," the detective remarked thoughtfully as he stared in the direction the hansom had gone. A moment later, he had recovered his equanimity. "I tell you what, old man. Unless I am much mistaken, by now Lestrade and his herd of elephants have obtained a warrant and have trampled the premises of the late Rupert Milestone."

"They won't find the paintings," I said.

"Nor will they," he agreed, pursing his lips. "But what *will* they unearth?"

"The hidden banknotes?"

"Very good, Watson. I think it will prove instructive to learn if they have. Do you think we might flag a cabbie who has no thought of murdering me?" He favored me with an enigmatic smile. "By the by, did you notice Signor Garibaldi's fingernails?"

"There were coloured flecks of paint under several."

"An authenticator's occupational hazard, I expect. Good, again, Watson. Really, you are coming along. Cabbie!"

Holmes's prophecy about the police ransacking Rupert Milestone's flat proved correct, but the circumstances under which we learned this were rather different than he'd foreseen.

Hardly had we alighted at 221 when an agitated Mrs. Hudson met us at the door and handed the detective a note. "The man was all in a lather not to find you here," she said as Holmes tore open the envelope.

"Hullo, this is peculiar," he said.

"What is?"

"My powers of prognostication. It's from Lady Glendenning, asking us to join her at Turncoat Lane as soon as possible. Cabbie, wait here! I'll just be a moment and we'll be off again."

He returned shortly, clutching the carpet bag we had employed earlier, and climbed in beside me.

"What do you imagine has happened?" I wondered as the vehicle made an awkward turn and began its clattering journey west.

The detective shook his head. "Could we have missed something on the premises? I find that hard to believe, but," he conceded with a philosophical shrug, "I've been wrong before."

When we reached Notting Hill shortly after six, a crowd had congregated outside number 2, held in check by yet another police barrier. Recognized on sight, Holmes and I were passed through and escorted into the painter's studio, where, as Holmes anticipated, Gregson's crew appeared to be making a mess of things.

In this he proved mistaken. The mess had in fact taken place before the arrival of the police. The front door lock had been smashed and the place turned upside down in a fashion even the forces of law and order could not have managed.

Inspector Gregson was clearly relieved to see us. "Someone's broken in and burgled the place," he explained soberly. "Not a lot to be seen," he added, clearly desirous of being contradicted by Holmes and increasing his scanty store of knowledge.

Holmes cast his eye at the unfolding chaos. "I shouldn't think so under the circumstances," he said dryly. "Is anything conspicuously missing?"

"Well, not that we—that is—"

"I thought as much. Where is Lady Glendenning?"

"In the pantry. The poor lady appears to be in a state of—well, seems a bit—"

"Thank you, Inspector."

We strode past the big man and into the vaulted studio. The snow above the skylight had melted and the large space now could easily be made out in its entirety. Someone had thrown aside the drop cloth from the easel and the Venetian scene remained where we had left it, the absence of gesso on its unpainted portion seemingly having proved of no interest to Gregson or his men.

Lady Glendenning was seated on a kitchen chair, staring vacantly into space. She had removed her hat and set it on her lap. Her flaxen hair was gathered into a severe knot.

"Lady Glendenning?"

It took the woman several seconds before she registered her name. She blinked from her trance and responded in a flat voice.

"Mr. Holmes. Dr. Watson. How do you come to be here?"

"You sent for us," Holmes reminded her.

Again there followed a curious lapse of time before she responded. "Did I? Yes, I suppose I did. I'm not sure why. The police sent for me but I'm not sure what they imagine I can tell them. So I sent for you. It's just that . . . This,"—she gestured to the shambles—"all this—it's not over, is it?"

"I believe I warned you it probably wasn't," Holmes said gently.

"It appears there has been a robbery." She gestured again at the chaos of men and upended furniture with the air of someone numbed by ill fortune.

"What has been taken?" Holmes followed her look.

"Some clothing is all, apparently, they tell me." The lady wrung her hands as I had seen her do on an earlier occasion. "Oh, I do wish Basil were here. He would know what to do."

"Dr. Watson and I will have a look, if you've no objection." There was a dull nod and the vacant stare resumed as we passed into the bedroom.

With rapid gestures, Holmes felt inside the shoes and passed a hand beneath the heavy mattress, eyeing me meaningfully as he came up empty-handed. "I see the linen chest has been opened, Inspector."

"Yes, we forced the lock."

"The lock was intact?"

"It was."

The detective appeared surprised. "And what did you find?"

The inspector threw his arms wide. "Nothing worth locking, Mr. Holmes, that is certain. A lot of bedding, some of it moth-eaten."

"No clothing belonging to a woman?"

Gregson's eyes widened. "How did you come to know we found women's garments, sir, if I may ask."

"You may ask," Holmes said, smiling. "And how much money did your men find?"

"Money?" The policeman frowned. "In the chest?"

"Anywhere on the premises," amended the detective.

The man's perplexity increased. "We've found no money. Not a brass farthing, Mr. Holmes."

"Not under the mattress? Nor stashed in a shoe? One hesitates to suggest, Inspector, but I would hope that no one under your direction can be accused of possessing sticky fingers."

Gregson stiffened. "Mr. Holmes, I'll have you know my men are members of the Metropolitan Police. If anything of value has turned up—or does turn up—you will be sure to learn of it."

"I stand corrected, Inspector."

"There is one thing I forgot to pass on," the policeman said. "I didn't think it terribly important at the time, but since you place such store in trifles—"

"What is it?" The detective strove to keep the impatience out of his voice.

"Well, it's to do with the corpse of the late Rupert Milestone—"

"Has someone called to claim the body?"

"Nothing so convenient, I fear, but the snow had completely melted by the time the body reached the coroner's and Mr. Brownlow and his boys were surprised to see there were no shoes."

"What?"

"The man was fully clothed and in his stocking feet but with no sign of abandoned footwear anywhere in Kensington Gardens."

Holmes passed a hand over his mouth. "The feet were bare?"

"Except for his hose, yes. Black silk with embroidered gold clocks."

Holmes contemplated this. "Many thanks, Inspector Gregson."

"Thought it might be a clue you'd know what to make of, Mr. Holmes."

The detective did not trouble to respond to this belated acknowledgement of his abilities.

"Where is the body now, Inspector?"

"Abney Park Cemetery, Indigents' Section. There wasn't much left of the poor man—my, but he did smell sweet."

Holmes chose to ignore the policeman's notion of humor.

"What are we do make of that?" I asked. "If the shoes were, as we've seen, made by Canons, perhaps the killer sought them for himself?"

This elicited a mordant smile. "We know Milestone's assailant was also furnished with expensive shoes—from Kirbys, as I recall. And while some people (including murderers, for all I know), may make a fetish of footwear, his killer, we have established, had his hands, rather than his feet, full."

"But you have said that anomalies such as the victim's missing shoes are not to be ignored."

"I do not propose to ignore this one," Holmes answered. "Perhaps Lady Glendenning may shed some light on the question."

"She's gone 'ome," a policeman explained when we asked after Lady Glendenning. "Said to thank you for coming, Mr. 'olmes."

"Small wonder," I said. "The woman looked as though she'd been run down by this afternoon's cabbie."

Outside Milestone's studio, it was past four and we turned up our collars against the chill.

"That was illuminating," I said. "No banknotes found."

"Always assuming Gregson's men are as upright as the policeman's chorus in *The Pirates of Penzance*," Holmes replied, "but there's no way of knowing for a certainty. There was a great deal of money in that studio when last we were there and now there appears to be none. As Macbeth says, 'Who so firm that cannot be seduced?'"*

"If not a bobby on the take, it would seem the robber discovered it."

"A robber who knew what he was looking for. According to Gregson, the lock on the linen chest was intact until the police forced it. And the lingerie was still there."

---

*   Macbeth says nothing of the kind. Cassius says it in another play.

"Suggesting the thief knew not to trouble himself about the contents of the chest?"

"Or herself, Watson. We mustn't exclude the possibility that the burglar was female."

"The nude whose portrait we found in the linen chest?"

"A possibility that must be considered."

"I find it difficult to imagine a woman smashing the front door lock," I confessed.

"I don't," said the detective. "The most winning woman of my acquaintance was capable of prodigious feats of strength."

"Holmes, the bearded lady at Chipperfields is not a fair example."*

"I think we are straying from the point, Watson."

There I was forced to agree with him. "But as the whole place was turned topsy-turvy, the thief clearly didn't know what to look for or where to look for it. Possibly by the time he—or she—reached the linen chest he—or she—had run out of time," I suggested.

"Possibly." But Holmes did not sound like a man convinced. "Altogether a queer sort of burglary," he murmured looking about. "Someone in need of clothes and money. One lock smashed and another left intact." He looked around. "What has become of our cab?"

Once more in Baker Street, I watched uneasily as Holmes tacked up our stolen canvases. The unvarnished Rembrandt he affixed to the top and bottom of the frame encompassing our picture of General Gordon. Milestone's nude he boldly tacked onto the wall

---

* Chipperfields was a well-known circus.

above our hearth, previously embellished by bullet pocks spelling out the initials of the Queen.

"I say Holmes, we can't have that thing in plain view. Mrs. Hudson will have heart failure."

"Mrs. Hudson will have to lump it, I fear," the detective replied. "These two items constitute additional clues."

"In a case on which we're no longer working, I remind you."

"Ah, Watson, have you no definition of the word 'amateur'?"

"Dilettante?" I hazarded.

"One who works for love of the work. Come, don't you think our rooms look better for a bit of art on the walls, and one of them a Rembrandt?"

"A possible Rembrandt."

He smiled. "But if one can't tell the difference, what *is* the difference?"

"She'll prefer your old bullet pocks," I mumbled.

We stared in silence for several moments at the two pictures, one old, the other unmistakably modern. Genuine or not, the Rembrandt, as Signor Garibaldi said, was brilliant. Without its sheen of varnish, the golden self-portrait nonetheless glowed with the painter's unique intensity, while the nude's blue-eyed stare held me in its unabashed gaze.

Holmes remained silent, his eyes swiveling in contemplation between the images.

"Holmes, what about tomorrow?"

He looked at me. "Tomorrow?"

"Yes, what is to be our next move?"

"Watson, I am delighted to learn you have decided to accept amateur status." He thought for a moment before smiling. "The next move in question will be yours, my boy."

"I beg your pardon?"

"Tomorrow, might I prevail upon you to call at Packwood's?"

"The art gallery? Certainly, but why?"

"Did you not recall someone of that name in your old regiment?"

"Yes, but—"

"The fair sex is your bailiwick, old man. My impression is that the fetching Miss Packwood with whom I spoke, interrogated under some plausible pretext, might reveal a great deal to a subtle inquisitor about the likes of Signor Garibaldi and Sir Johnny Van Dam."

"I will do my best."

"I know you will succeed."

"And you?"

Still smiling, he hefted the carpet bag.

"What have you there?"

His smile broadened. "Phenol and formaldehyde, pinched from Milestone's flat, which Gregson and his crew will never miss. I think the time has come to return to my first love."

Love was not a word Holmes often used, but I rose to the challenge.

"Chemistry?"

"Very good, Watson. Yes, chemistry."

7

CHEMISTRY

"May I assist you?" inquired the young lady behind the desk at Packwood's. I experienced an unaccustomed sensation the instant I set eyes on her. Tall, with a willowy figure, she looked much as Holmes had described. Smartly but demurely attired in mauve with a touch of white at her wrists and throat, her aspect was alert and businesslike, yet a suggestion of merriment sparkling in her eyes hinted at a cheerful disposition. But there was something else, an aura that jolted me to my core. I had planned to feign awkwardness, but abruptly realized there was no need.

"I confess I'm not quite sure. Miss Packwood? Are you she?"

"I am Juliet Packwood, yes," she answered, smiling. "What is it you'd care to see? Perhaps I can help. Seascapes or some still lifes? We have—"

"To be truthful, I am not much of an art . . ." I trailed off as if in search of a word which she was eager to supply.

"Connoisseur?"

"Well—"

"Collector? Aficionado?"

"Afi—?"

"Art lover?" Her smile broadened.

"I *like* art—" I was fumbling in earnest now.

"Are you here under duress? Has the little woman insisted?" She was laughing, then looked guiltily about to make sure she'd not been overheard. "*Mea culpa*," she lowered her voice to a conspiratorial whisper. "Uncle Gerald is always telling me that in this business one must appear dignified and somehow superior, but some days I simply can't seem to manage it." She looked over her shoulder again at half a dozen art lovers, gazing in respectful silence at the pictures on display and sighed. "This appears to be one of those days."

"I know what you mean," I responded, lowering my voice to match hers. "I'm a doctor and some days, listening to my hypochondriacs, it's all I can do to keep a straight face."

"So it seems we are contrarians," she whispered back.

"Not necessarily," I parried, which prompted a chortle.

Then in a normal tone, as if recollecting the dignity the place and her post demanded, she asked, "Please tell me what sort of pictures you're looking to see. We have some very fine—"

"I'm afraid I couldn't tell a Turner from a Tintoretto, Miss Packwood." I hoped I was able to manifest something like a blush. "In point of fact, I'm not really here to talk about pictures."

Miss Packwood frowned. "Not here for the pictures?" The frown quickly gave way to another of her beguiling smiles. "Sailing under false colours? What a pity, for my credentials are impeccable. I studied in Florence under Professor Berenson."*

"Ah, Professor Berenson," I repeated sagely, but this likewise failed to pass muster and prompted another smile.

"If not art, then what is it you wish to—?"

"The fact is I noticed the Packwood name outside as I was walking just now and it put me in mind of a chap I knew in the army years ago in Afghanistan—Jack Packwood?"

It was she who blushed, not I. "You knew my—may I ask, in which regiment did you serve?"

"Fifth Northumberland Fusiliers. I realize the chances are small but I thought perhaps there might be some connection."

More colour rose to those cheeks. "You are speaking of my late father, Colonel John Packwood. He was killed at Maiwand."

"I am so sorry. I was at Maiwand. Your father was an excellent soldier. Were you close?"

"I scarcely knew him," the young woman said, eyes brimming now. "I had just turned seven when we were informed of his death."

"I am so sorry," I repeated. In this I was telling the truth as I could see mention of her father had distressed her. "Are you all right, Miss Packwood? I had no desire to—"

"What was he like, Mister—"

---

* If true, Juliet Packwood's credentials were impressive. Bernard Berenson's expertise was manifest in *Venetian Painters of the Renaissance* (1894), *Florentine Painters of the Renaissance* (1896), and *Central Italian Painters of the Renaissance* (1897), among others. He curated for Isabella Stewart Gardner in Boston.

"Doctor," I reminded her. "Doctor Hamish Watson."

"What was my father like, Dr. Watson?"

"An excellent soldier, as I have said—"

"Besides that."

I stole a look at the art lovers admiring the pictures in the small gallery. "I've no wish to distract your clientele. Might I suggest somewhere nearby for a cup of tea at a convenient time? It might be a more suitable place to converse."

She followed my look, satisfied potential buyers were gliding sedately from one canvas to the next, then returned her attention to me. Juliet Packwood's physiognomy was wonderfully expressive. She looked me up and down, making up her mind. I withstood her scrutiny as best I could. I knew she was taking inventory of a professional man of less than forty, of medium height, with a full head of graying hair, neatly trimmed moustache, and a slight limp. Holmes doubtless would have seen and told her more. Merely examining my watch, he had deduced the unhappy history of my elder brother. As Miss Packwood broke into another of her smiles, I could only be thankful he wasn't here to enlighten her.

"In one hour? There's a tearoom just 'round the corner. Percy will man the fort."

"In one hour, Miss Packwood." It would give me time to think up tales of a man I had scarcely known.

I was early for our meeting, smoking and unable to take my eyes from the tearoom door. The hour passed interminably and I grew to loathe the tingle of the overhead bell that rang maddeningly at every entrance and exit. Five minutes after the appointed time, the wretched bell finally tolled for me and Miss Packwood emerged beneath it. She had no difficulty seeing me as I rose to greet her.

"I hope I've not kept you waiting." In this light I could see her delicate features were embellished by a sprinkling of freckles.

"Not a bit of it." I soon found myself seated opposite the young woman, stirring my third cup of tea and trying to satisfy her curiosity about her father without entirely annihilating the ninth commandment.

"I didn't know him well," I began. "I was an army surgeon in my twenties, you understand, only just down from Netley and surgeons are not, as a rule, on familiar terms with senior officers, except of course, in the unhappy event—" I could see this was heading into sensitive territory and altered course. "The colonel, of course, was rather older than I—"

"What was he like?" She was on fire to learn about her father, while I was conflicted about supplying information I didn't possess and found myself reluctant to manufacture. Before meeting her, obeying Holmes's instructions to learn about Sir Johnny had been merely another assignment among dozens I had carried out during the many years of our association. I had spotted the nearby teashop well before entering Packwood's. But confronted by my quarry in person (I dared not tell myself in the flesh), my errand abruptly threatened to become an entirely different proposition.

"Oh, hard to say, but well-liked. He loved a joke. Had a ready laugh . . ."

"Oh." Clearly this was not how Miss Packwood remembered her father, or had been led to picture him.

"Of course he had a serious side," I added quickly. "Something of a deep thinker, I should say."

She nodded with satisfaction. This appeared more to conform to her mental image of the man. "Did you see him die?"

Here I was on solid ground. "I did not. As a matter of fact, I was almost killed myself during the battle—"

"Heavens!" Her dark eyes shone with sympathy.

"Struck by a jezail bullet." This again was true. "Only saved by my orderly. Maiwand was an appalling business. I am lucky to have survived and can only extend belated condolences on behalf of your unfortunate father. Did I understand you to say his brother runs the gallery?"

It took Juliet Packwood some moments to regain her composure but she was not maudlin by nature and allowed herself to be diverted in this simple fashion.

"Yes, Uncle Gerald has made a go of it. We're nothing like the big places, of course, but we do a steady business, especially among country gentry who think they must have something to fill blank places on their walls when they come up to town. I daresay we're an afterthought, once they've visited Fortnum's." She expressed this without rancor.

"And you're in a smart neighborhood, to be sure. Nothing like Van Dam's, but—"

"Oh, Van Dam's." She rolled her eyes and laughed. "If those pictures could talk!"

"How do you mean?" I signaled for more tea.

"Most of it is gossip to be sure, but even if half were true—"

"I have a weakness for gossip," I confided, adopting once more the conspiratorial tone that she evidently found amusing.

"Really, I oughtn't to be telling tales out of school."

"School is far off," I urged. "Have you ever crossed paths with Lord Southbank? One hears so much about the man. Are those stories true? Is he really all they say?"

She was on the point of answering but apparently thought better of it and bit her lip. I waited, occupying myself by squeezing lemon into my tea. After a lengthy pause and choosing her words with care, she attempted to satisfy my curiosity, speaking in a somewhat formal vein.

"Let us merely stipulate that we are in effect talking about two persons, Sir Johnny and Lord Southbank. Underneath his beaming aura of hail-fellow-well-met, Sir Johnny is far from the jovial entrepreneur he makes himself out to be. One doesn't cross Lord Southbank lightly," she added, frowning.

"Do you speak from experience?" I regretted the words the instant they left my mouth. The sight of her distress gave me a pang. "I'm sorry. I didn't mean to pry."

She shrugged and, like me, sought refuge fidgeting with her tea. Again I chose not to interrupt her thoughts and was treated to another protracted silence during which she evidently wrestled with conflicting impulses. I increasingly hated those false colours under which she had intuited I was sailing. Juliet Packwood deserved better.

"There's all sorts of rumors about Sir Johnny," she said, addressing the teacup. "When he speaks, you know at once he's not English.

His origins are obscure. I've heard he's Dutch or something, started on the streets in Brussels selling bric-a-brac and went from there. This much is common knowledge," she added as if to satisfy herself that in speaking of matters already on the record, she was guilty of no impropriety.

"Quite an ascent."

She did not smile. "He's certainly found his niche. Sir Johnny's specialty is selling old master portraits of young women to rich, childless, widowers," she resumed at length.

This was precisely the sort of information Holmes had instructed me to obtain. "Paintings of young women sold to rich widowers. What a curious line of country."

"But very lucrative, doctor."

"Are there so many rich widowers then?"

"Or to wealthy bachelors with an eye for a pretty face," she went on, warming to her theme. "Single men, old or young, are susceptible to such iconography. Perhaps, on occasion, married ones as well. Oh, he's clever, is Sir Johnny. A psychologist of the trade, you might say." She flashed her remarkable smile before just as quickly revoking it. "What is less well-known is the fact that if the women in those pictures are not sufficiently young or sufficiently attractive, if they are wearing too many clothes, if one's eyes are judged the wrong colour for the buyer's preference or another could do with a more agreeable nose, if a third needs an asset, a glistening pearl earring, let us say—any or all these defects are discreetly remedied in Sir Johnny's workshop."

"His workshop?"

"Van Dam's maintains a staff of what are termed 'preservationists.' And, as I have reason to know, they do more than 'preserve.'"

"My word! Is that—how to put this—legal?" I thought it wiser not to inquire too quickly into her offhand suggestion of personal knowledge. I would work up to that on another occasion. I was already thinking of other occasions.

Unaware of my strategizing, she offered another shrug. "There are few rules in the world of art, doctor."

"You amaze me, Miss Packwood."

Again she was silent. Was she regretting her confidences? I began to fear our exchanges were losing momentum. Rather than allow this, I opened another line of inquiry.

"Has anyone ever seen this preservation workshop? I imagine it must be quite a sight, an old master factory."

She smiled again, though it was clear her amusement was tinged with other emotions. "Oh, I doubt the place you describe is situated on the premises. Sir Johnny would keep his hands as clean as Pilate's and would not be so foolish as to sully them with paint, but in this world, while there may be no laws, it is nonetheless hard to keep secrets. Word gets around. You know how it is."

"I suppose that would explain Rupert Milestone," I ventured.

This was a blunder. The young woman's eyes narrowed.

"What do you know of Rupert Milestone? You are the second person in as many days inquiring after him."

"I'm not inquiring in the least," I hastened to say, my mind racing to anticipate her inevitable next question.

"But you know him."

"By reputation only. A former patient has spoken of him to me. Her late husband owned a great deal of property in town which his widow must now administer and this Milestone was—*is*," I corrected myself, hoping she wouldn't notice my alteration, "one of her tenants." I could only hope word of the painter's death had not yet appeared in the papers. "The patient has spoken with some admiration of his pictures and said something about his connection with Van Dam's."

She sniffed at this intelligence before returning to the subject of Colonel Packwood, at which point further tarradiddles were in order before I escorted her back to the gallery.

"Thank you so much for telling me about my father," she said, taking my hand in hers and pressing it earnestly. "You've opened a window on a past that is almost entirely closed to me."

"Miss Packwood," I said, returning the pressure, "I only wish I had more to tell you, though it's possible, now you've prompted my memory, that with time, additional details may come to mind. Might I call upon you again?"

I had not thought to say these words. They had simply popped out of my mouth.

Juliet Packwood cocked her head and regarded me, once more smiling with the expression that so became her.

"You might," she said, before disappearing into Packwood's, taking her smile with her.

I decamped to Baker Street, my thoughts in a whirl. That smile was like seeing the world illumined by lightning. When it vanished everything became dull again. I found myself wondering if that smile was among Juliet Packwood's arsenal of feminine wiles. Was

I succumbing to Holmes's chronic suspicion of women? It was not an agreeable thought.

In the entryway I was accosted by Mrs. Hudson. "I think Mr. Holmes has gone mad," she greeted me, pointing up the stairs.

Had she already been scandalized by the nude over our hearth?

"Holmes? Mad in what way?" By now I was certainly used to the detective's eccentricities.

"You'll see. Do be careful, doctor."

Not knowing what to expect, I trudged up the stairs inhaling, as I did so, the pleasing scent of linseed oil which grew more pronounced as I opened our door.

"Holmes what are you doing?"

The detective greeted me with a smile of his own, which did not compare with Miss Packwood's, being distinctly pawky with a satisfied smugness thrown in. Our two purloined pictures remained where he had mounted them, but his newfound obsession had expanded, for he was wearing a smock, holding a palette and paintbrush, and standing before an easel on which a small, blank canvas had been secured by the top clamp.

"I thought I might take up painting, my dear fellow. Do I look the part?"

"You look absurd." He seemed indifferent to this and to the fact that our sitting room was a shambles once more.

"Good news, Watson. I've managed to concoct gesso—it's rather a messy business and I'm sorry to report there's a bit of egg on your chair, but after several attempts I believe I've mastered the formula."

"Holmes, really—"

"Now we must wait for the stuff to cure before making a start. While we do, tell me of your encounter with Miss Packwood."

Suppressing my annoyance, I related what I had learned, after which I sank into my egg-stained chair, suddenly exhausted. He regarded me with concern.

"You did well, Watson. Watson?"

I found I was unable to answer.

"Watson?"

"Sorry. I was just thinking."

"What about?"

I looked up at my friend, wondering how much I should say.

The detective's eyes twinkled. "Oh, I see."

"But I did obtain the information for which you asked," I protested.

"So you did, old man. Lord Southbank's business increasingly comes to resemble something perilously close to a swindle."

"As Miss Packwood describes it, matters certainly appear black against him," I agreed. "Holmes, what is the object of this latest mania?"

He laughed in his silent fashion. "Not to see if I've inherited any of the Vernet talent, I assure you." He set down a sable-haired brush. "I am trying to supplement the knowledge I gleaned all those years ago at the British Museum and understand other attributes of oil paint." With a sweep of his hand, he indicated several new paint tubes I recognized as similar to those I had seen near Rupert Milestone's easel.

"In days of yore, doctor, painters were obliged to concoct needed colours on the spot by blending minerals and ores with various oils. Safflower, linseed, poppy, walnut, or lilac oils were employed on an ad hoc basis, rather akin to chefs' recipes, but starting a century or so ago in France, a certain Monsieur Lefranc began offering oil-based paint in tubes for commercial sale with ingenious screw caps of the sort we now take for granted. Nowadays the company that emblazons his name on every tube has several competing imitators, enabling any man aspiring to be the next Da Vinci to try his hand. Watson, where are you going?"

"Out. Holmes, we've only just managed to air out the place."

"Will you bring back a sausage roll?" he called after me.

And so began a considerable alteration in our routine. I continued to cultivate Juliet Packwood, telling myself it was my obligation to learn more about the business of art and Lord Southbank's swindle (as Holmes characterized it), knowing all the while my motives had nothing to do with either. On the occasion when I first fled our rooms, Holmes had acceded to my complaints by opening the windows so that by the time of my return (with the desired sausage roll), the place was freezing. During my absence he had painted several squares, each a different colour, over the hardened gesso. He was now employing a Bunsen burner like a blowtorch to attack his artwork.

"May I please close the windows? I shall catch my death."

"Close them by all means, my dear fellow. My, but you are changeable."

I wasted no time slamming them shut. "What are you attempting, may I ask? Are these splotches some form of modern art? If so, I don't believe it will catch on."

"I am trying to solve the problem of drying oil paint quickly." He turned off the flame. "It's no use. These swatches merely blister instead of hardening, just like this one." He held up the swatch of burnt canvas he had taken from the kiln in Rupert Milestone's studio with its spot of scorched purple. "Even oil of lilac, which, I've discovered, has the highest boiling point, blisters rather than hardens." He shook his head. "That was what the kiln must have been for." He peeled off the smock, absently allowing it to fall to the floor.

"Stop a bit. Are you saying that Rupert Milestone was some sort of accomplice?"

"I think it highly probable. He was by, Miss Packwood's account, something of an artistic chameleon, able to replicate innumerable styles. Perhaps he began innocently enough as a mere restorer, retouching torn canvases and so forth, but it was only a matter of time before Sir Johnny noticed and found a use for the man's peculiar gifts, with compensation of some sort, to be sure. This might serve to explain a wardrobe tailored in Savile Row. But for his handiwork to pass muster, the paint would have to dry lest so little as a pin wielded by a suspicious authenticator give the game away. Hence the business with the kiln. When that didn't solve the problem, he had it disconnected, doubtless to lower the gas bill."

Retaining my coat, I sank into my chair. "I don't understand. Surely if a collector buys a painting it would not astonish him to learn the image has undergone some minor 'preservation'—a scratched canvas retouched, a fresh application of varnish and so forth. No one would expect the restored portion to be as hard as the rest, especially if the painting in question had been vetted by Signor Garibaldi or another such authority to the buyer's satisfaction."

"Yes, but Signor Garibaldi and others of his ilk would also need to be compensated for their participation in the scheme," Holmes realized. He stretched out on the day bed, hands locked behind his neck, and stared at the ceiling. "It's a jigsaw puzzle, Watson. There are many pieces, possibly too many pieces"—he jerked his head in the direction of Milestone's nude and Rembrandt's self-portrait—"but they must fit together somehow to yield a complete image."

"Would one of those missing pieces include the dead painter's missing shoes?"

He eyed me from his recumbent posture. "It would." He volunteered no more but continued to stare at the ceiling.

"Tomorrow I am taking Miss Packwood to the zoo, Holmes."

Lost in thought, the detective did not answer.

"Do you think they are content?"

Juliet Packwood posed this question as we observed the lions on their island confinement in the heart of London. I was more concerned by the width of the moat that separated the beasts from onlookers like ourselves. I didn't relish the prospect of these carnivores in close proximity, especially to the woman with whom I had rapidly become smitten.

"I expect it's a question of how much they recall of their former lives."

"You mean before captivity?"

"Something like that."

"I should like to see the elephants."

I had thought the Regent's Park Zoo would prove a pleasant outing but this afternoon, unlike our previous excursions, Juliet Packwood seemed distracted.

"By all means." We strolled in afternoon sunshine to where the pachyderms occupied an island of their own.

"Are these Indian or African elephants, do you know?"

"Indian, without question."

"What makes you so certain?" Her voice sounded distant, as if her thoughts were elsewhere and her questions merely pro forma conversational gambits.

"Indian elephants are smaller, have much smaller ears, and can be domesticated. Your African species is wild, much bigger, with enormous ears, and exceedingly dangerous."

She made no comment on this. From there we visited the reptile house, darkened and heated to accommodate the slithery creatures. My companion shuddered as she observed a dozing cobra.

"It looks benign," she murmured, "without its flaring hood."

"I saw them in India," I remembered. "They are only surpassed for toxicity by the swamp adder, sometimes known as the speckled band."

"Is the swamp adder only to be found in India?" I found her soft voice in the darkness distinctly ominous.

"As a rule, but the one I encountered was here in England,"* I responded. "Come, let's see the monkeys," but she refused to take her eyes off the snake.

---

* For Watson's full account of this horrific experience, the reader is referred to "The Adventure of the Speckled Band."

"Tell me, doctor—"

"Hamish, please."

"Doctor," she firmly insisted. "Have you seen this morning's paper?"

"I'm not sure I know what you—"

"Artist Murdered!" Her raised voice echoed in the confined space, startling those nearby. She continued, speaking more quietly, "The newsboys are hawking it in the streets this morning. The artist in question has been identified."

"Oh?"

"Surely you know, doctor. As Rupert Milestone."

"Rupert—Oh."

She turned in the darkness and faced me. Without being able to see, I knew she was not smiling. "Do you believe in coincidence, doctor? I do not."

"I'm sure I have no—"

"If you are not prepared to be truthful, let us return to Packwood's. I've had enough of snakes, speckled or otherwise."

It was impossible to miss her meaning. She walked before me and I followed in chastened silence. What ought I to say to her?

"Miss Packwood, I confess my initial visit to you was not a coincidence," I said as we emerged from the zoo.

"Were you ever at Maiwand? Did you even know my father?"

"I most certainly was and I most certainly did know him!" I protested vehemently. "And I most definitely almost lost my life at Maiwand! Feel free to check the Army Lists. Please let me explain."

"I am not going to take more tea with you, doctor."

"Then I will offer my explanation here in Prince Albert Road." This I proceeded to do, speaking quickly, my breath coming in all the wrong places so that I gasped throughout my recital. Juliet Packwood listened in sullen silence while I told her of Holmes and Lady Glendenning. "I told you the truth about her, as well," I insisted, "though not by name. Rupert Milestone was her tenant."

"Sherlock Holmes?" She appeared to be having difficulty following my disjointed sentences.

"Yes! You met him."

"I did no such thing."

"Forgive me, Miss Packwood, but you did. He told you his name was Jasper Gilmore when he called at your gallery."

She frowned. "Mr. Gilmore is an American."

I sighed. "You were deceived by an accomplished actor, Miss Packwood."

She fixed me with a look. "*That* was Sherlock Holmes? *The* Sherlock Holmes? And I suppose you are *the* Dr. Watson? The Dr. Watson whose accounts appear in *The Strand Magazine* where I imagine they are to be found in barber shops and doctors' waiting rooms?"

"Yes." I chose to ignore her condescending description. "Sherlock Holmes and I are searching for Rupert Milestone's murderer. I told you the truth so far as we thought prudent. Please believe me. You must believe me."

She regarded me with those jet eyes as I babbled. At once exasperated and indecisive, the young woman appeared to be reeling under a succession of blows. When I had finished, or rather, run out of breath, we stood facing one another.

"Is your real name Hamish?"

"Hamish is my middle name. My Christian name is John."

"I pity any man called John," she said, addressing the pavement.

"Please tell me what you are thinking, Miss Packwood. Now that I've told you the truth, I hope you don't think less of me."

She surveyed me up and down. "I couldn't possibly think less of you, doctor."

"But—"

"I am thinking about what I am thinking," she said before turning on her heel and striding purposefully away.

"Will I see you again?" I called after her. She did not answer and I knew better than to pursue her. I made my way back to Baker Street, my heart heavy with the thought that I might never behold that smile again.

8

CARROTS & STICKS

"Holmes, is that atrocious smell formaldehyde?" My voice was strident with upset upon my return. "This place reeks like a mortuary!"

"A formaldehyde mixture, yes. Forgive me, my dear fellow." The detective was huddled over his chemical apparatus with predictably odiferous results.

"Insupportable! What in heaven's name can you be doing?"

"Trying to understand what phenol and formaldehyde have to do with one another and where paint comes into the business." As he spoke he was rinsing crucibles, pipettes, beakers, and test tubes. Preoccupied by these tasks he mercifully failed to detect my miserable state. "Forgive the stench, my dear fellow. Let us open the windows and go out for fresh air."

"Out? Where? I've only just—"

"To Portobello Road."

"Portobello Road?"

He laid a hand on my shoulder. "Watson, you must rid yourself of the habit of echoing my last sentences."

"Answer my question," I fumed. "Why are you now bent on going to Portobello Road?"

"It's Saturday. The antique stalls will be open and I must buy a painting."

"Painting? What sort of painting?"

He favored me with a rueful expression. "An expensive one—but then we've Lady Glendenning's cheque on deposit to pay for it."

I accompanied him. Any errand, no matter how pointless, was preferable to staying alone in our fetid rooms, nursing a broken heart like some lovesick schoolboy. In addition to my misery, I was aware of a certain stupefaction that, after all this time as a widower, I could be so suddenly overcome by an emotion I had long since thought dead.

Portobello Road was indeed bustling on this Saturday afternoon. Spring was finally in the air and the sun shone brightly as Holmes and I ambled through a cornucopia of treasure and bric-a-brac, some in open shops and windows, the rest on display under tenting in the road. Sellers hawked willow pattern china, chipped porcelain teacups with gold filigree, Wedgwood soup bowls, and pewter tankards alongside sterling cutlery and flatware. There were sets of painted lead soldiers, some missing heads or arms. Nestled in frayed velvet-lined boxes were medals attached to faded ribbons, some from the Crimea and even Waterloo. In addition, retrieved from obscure garrets, were paintings on tattered canvas, many twisted on warped stretchers. Everything to be seen was there to be haggled over. Confronted by such intriguing miscellany, it was easy for me to forget the purpose of our errand and revert to my own unhappy state, dully picking over useless nonsense, the more so as the detective had declined to enlighten me as to the object of our search.

"Watson, don't dally. I shall misplace you in this throng."

I reluctantly abandoned my rabbit hole and tagged after Holmes who looked at and spurned several indifferent daubs before finding one that commanded his attention.

"Holmes, that is nothing worth your time."

"Perhaps not. But put a frame around it and it becomes art," he mused. "Collectors labor under an illusion, Watson."

"How do you mean?"

He held the picture at arm's length, turning it this way and that in the afternoon light. "When we buy a picture or statue we imagine we own it," he said as he turned to face me, "but in reality the reverse is true. The picture now owns *us*. We are in fact mere custodians, hostages to its safekeeping. We must shelter and care for it, for it turns out it belongs not to us but to posterity."

"This?" I gestured to the canvas.

"Well," he smiled, "perhaps not this, but you see what I'm getting at."

"I do." I found myself beguiled for the moment, challenged by the detective's theory. "I confess a version of the thought crossed my mind some time ago, when you spoke of paintings being at the mercy of war and tear."

But Holmes was out of earshot, having wandered several paces ahead.

"Hullo, what have we here?" He held up a canvas in better condition and turned to the seller, a slovenly Scot with imposing red eyebrows who was absorbed by his newspaper and cigarette. The man glanced up briefly.

"Hondius, squire," was the indifferent reply. "Hunting scene."

"What year? Do you know?"

The Scot now troubled himself to regard the detective and briefly reacquaint himself with the item on offer. "Dutch. Seventeenth century. You can just make out the signature."

"How much?"

A look of low cunning animated the features of the seller.

"Thirty guineas?"

"I'll take it."

The man blinked in mild surprise.

"Holmes you've been diddled," I said when we'd returned to Baker Street. "Why lay out a small fortune for this thing which you might easily have bartered down to half the man's asking price?"

"I hadn't the time," responded Holmes as he laid the painting in a cleared space on his chemical table and, with a small pincers, set about removing the nails that fastened the canvas to its stretcher.

"What on earth are you doing?"

"A small experiment." To my surprise, he produced the pumice stone he had filched from Rupert Milestone's studio and now began rubbing it delicately back and forth over the image.

"Holmes, you're destroying that picture!"

"I don't find it a very good picture, Watson. You said yourself with a bit of haggling I could have obtained it for half the price."

He was rubbing more vigorously now and the aged oil paint was flaking then vanishing under his efforts. "In any event," he added, wiping away the powdered detritus created by the stone with the back of his hand. "I needn't erase the whole image."

"You could have experimented on our Rembrandt," I said, rancorously, "and saved yourself thirty guineas."

"The Rembrandt is evidence." He continued scraping away at the paint. "There. What does that look like?"

"A desecration." I was still feeling sorry for myself.

He blew more paint dust away, exposing an inch or so of frayed, bare canvas.

"No, Watson, an inspiration. This looks like the empty bottom portion of the Venetian scene we saw on the easel at Rupert Milestone's studio. You will recall I discovered small granules of fine powder beneath the painting when I examined it."

I became curious despite myself. "You mean—"

He looked over at me, his gray eyes gleaming. "I mean that the Venetian cityscape we admired was not, as we first thought, unfinished."

"I'm not sure I—"

"It *was* finished, Watson!" The detective's voice vibrated with excitement. "*It was in the process of being erased!* The painting and the gesso beneath it. With this." He held up the pumice stone to explain how the feat was accomplished. "Resulting in the same white powder I discovered under my foot at the base of Milestone's easel."

"Erased? Whatever for?"

He stood away from the table and began filling his pipe. "Precisely. What for? Let us assume—and it is only an assumption at this point—that Milestone's intention was to eradicate the entire painting."

"That would merely leave a worthless old canvas."

"Old, certainly. But worthless? I am not sure. You will recall Mycroft telling me that old masters don't grow on trees. Following our assumption, that Milestone intended to pulverize the entire Venetian scene, had he finished, he would have had an authentic Renaissance canvas on which to create an entirely *new* old master, one possibly featuring an attractive young woman, rather than yet another view of Saint Marks."

We were interrupted by a knock on the door.

"What is it, Mrs. Hudson?"

Our landlady was holding a telegram. The detective held out his hand. "The telegram is addressed to Dr. Watson," she explained, giving it to me. Was it my imagination or did I detect a certain smugness in her reply?

If the detective was surprised, he concealed the fact, returning his attention to the canvas.

Trying to conceal my excitement, I tore open the envelope, then reached for my hat and coat. "Holmes, I must ask you to accompany me."

"I am presently engaged, as you see, my dear fellow." He was intently examining the space he had cleared of paint and gesso on the Hondius hunting scene.

"Holmes!" I said sternly, causing him to look up. "In our years together I have seldom asked you for anything and it may be fairly said I have toiled mightily on your behalf. Now I am asking for this." I handed him the telegram, which he read aloud:

"Meet me at the National Gallery at four. Stop. Bring your friend if he exists. Stop. J. P."

He looked from the telegram to the canvas, and finally, to me.

"I am asking you, Holmes."

There was a fractional pause.

"Of course, my dear man."

We arrived as Big Ben was tolling the hour. Juliet was waiting for us on the steps of the National Gallery, her tall, slender figure silhouetted before the imposing building.

"I hope I've not kept you waiting," said I, again breathless in her presence. "Miss Packwood, this is Jasper Gilmore of Topeka, Kansas, also known as Sherlock Holmes."

"Miss Packwood, I trust Dr. Watson has explained and apologized for our deception," Holmes began smoothly.

"Mr. Holmes, why did you not truthfully disclose your identity and explain the purpose of your visit at the outset when you came to me at Packwood's?" she demanded without acknowledging his greeting.

Holmes anticipated this question and had his answer in readiness. "I feared you might be reluctant to speak. You yourself said Lord Southbank is a dangerous man to cross. As Dr. Watson had served with your father in Afghanistan, it seemed wiser to let him approach the topic indirectly."

"And coax me into confidences." She favored me with an implacable stare, so different from her irresistible smile. I felt myself redden. "Lord Southbank *is* a dangerous man," she conceded before taking a breath. "Come, we've not much time before closing. Let us look at some pictures and I will explain more, though I'm not sure either of you deserve it."

Without waiting to see if we followed, she marched smartly up the steps and into the museum. Pausing only to exchange looks, the detective and I traipsed behind through a labyrinth of more art than I ever beheld in my life. The place seemed to go on for miles, conveying the curious impression the building was larger inside than out.

"When Henry VIII began the Protestant faith in order to obtain his divorce," Juliet Packwood began in the manner of a tour guide, speaking quietly over her shoulder, "he succeeded in cutting England off from Catholic Europe for nearly a hundred years. The unforeseen result was that England almost entirely missed the Renaissance."

I could see from the expression on Holmes's face as he regarded me, that this notion had never occurred to him, and I confess it came as news to me as well.

As she spoke, we passed pictures from various epochs and a bewildering array of styles. Even to my untutored eye, I understood I was looking at masterpieces produced in wide variety by other countries in other centuries.

"For the better part of a century, ergo, England knew nothing of Da Vinci, remained in ignorance of Raphael, Caravaggio, Titian, Rubens, Botticelli, or Michelangelo. All we had was Holbein the Younger," she concluded with a rueful expression, gesturing, as if on cue, to the German painter's portrait of stout King Henry.

"When relations between Protestant England and the Catholic Continent finally thawed, England began to see what she had missed. The reigning monarch, Charles I, most especially, became enamored of Renaissance nudes. Yes, naked women were purchased by the cartload from Italy by agents of His Majesty for his private apartments at Whitehall Palace, where only he could revel in them. The nucleus of what you see here in the National Gallery originated as Charles Stuart's private property."

"*Whose was it?*" murmured Holmes.

"*His who is gone,*" I responded automatically.

"I beg your pardon?" Juliet Packwood looked confused.

"It's rather a long story," Holmes replied. "As it happens I have crossed paths with Charles Stuart before."*

"How did the king's collection come to be here?" I interjected before Juliet could ask what was meant by this.

Miss Packwood, still in the impersonal manner of a docent, stopped and turned to address us. She had not been exaggerating her bona fides when she'd alluded to her Florentine studies.

"Since you claim some familiarity with the monarch, you know from your schoolboy history Charles I provoked a civil war which ended when Oliver Cromwell chopped off his head. The late king's art collection was now property of the Puritan Commonwealth, whose first impulse was to burn these impious images. But wiser, unsevered heads, prevailed. The civil war had bankrupted the country and it was thought the paintings' potential monetary value might help defray the expenses of the war. This may not have been history's first but was certainly its biggest art sale."

---

* For full details of this remarkable case (which Holmes related to Watson after the fact), the reader is referred to "The Adventure of the Musgrave Ritual." Holmes and Watson are here reciting from memory fragments of the tell-tale riddle whose cryptic questions and responses led to a sensational resolution.

She turned and resumed walking without waiting to enjoy our astonishment. "Here is a painting on wood by the Italian master, Botticelli. Do you observe anything unusual?"

The image was another provocative nude, but it took only moments to understand why she had halted before it.

"But," I stammered, "this woman—"

"Yes? What about her?" Miss Packwood crossed her arms.

This time I had no need to attempt a blush for I felt myself reddening. "This woman is you."

"The head only, you understand, certainly not the rest." She chose not to follow our gaze. "This was what I wished you to see and understand."

"But I don't understand in the least."

Holmes said nothing but continued to scrutinize the face in the painting.

"I believe I indicated I had some knowledge of Lord Southbank," said Juliet Packwood.

"Permit me to extrapolate," said Holmes, abruptly coming to life.

Her arms still forbiddingly folded, Juliet Packwood glanced at me. "I am eager to hear from Sherlock Holmes."

"This Botticelli was at one time in Sir Johnny's possession."

"It was."

"And he sold it to one of those rich, childless collectors who enjoy pictures of young women, as you described to Dr. Watson. Even as King Charles enjoyed such risqué images."

"He sold it, yes."

"And that same collector—or one of his heirs—eventually donated it here, to the National Gallery."

"Go on."

"But before the picture was offered to Van Dam's wealthy collector, it was thought that the young woman in the painting was—how shall I put this?—perhaps insufficiently attractive."

"Very good, Mr. Holmes. And so—?"

"And so you were approached by Sir Johnny and invited to model for his restorer."

"Which is how your face comes to be in the painting!" I ejaculated.

"It is." Juliet Packwood refrained from looking at me.

"May I ask, how was the invitation to model conveyed? Did Lord Southbank approach you directly?" asked Holmes.

Juliet Packwood took a breath. It was clear she was finally determined to reveal what she knew about Sir Johnny's scheme.

"Lord Southbank, in his boisterous Sir Johnny persona, is in the habit of poking his head into various galleries. Usually on Saturdays. 'Making his rounds,' he calls it, always laughing about seeing how the competition is faring, but in actuality I suspect he is looking for pictures to snap up for himself. 'Sleepers,' as they're sometimes termed in our trade, a painting whose owner has no understanding of its true worth. Knowledgeable gallerists buy them on the cheap, spruce them up with a fresh coat of varnish and fancy gilt frame, and they may fetch many times their original price."

"And on one of these occasions at Packwood's—" prompted Holmes.

"He bantered with my uncle in his usual fashion and then seemed to notice me. This was several years ago and I was quite young."

Holmes and I refrained from smiling at this.

"He glanced in my direction and said something like, 'I say, your niece is most becoming,' or some such folderol. 'My dear, would you have any interest in earning seven guineas for helping with a little restoration work? Nothing indecent, mind, just your face.' Well, you may imagine my delight. Seven guineas by my lights was—and is—a staggering sum, besides which, as a young woman, how could I help being flattered by an offer from such an important figure as Lord Southbank? Uncle Gerald looked less pleased but I now understand he was reluctant to cross Sir Johnny." She turned again to the painting. "And so there I am."

We gazed at the picture, now aware of its history, as our guide waited expectantly. The artist had even managed to replicate Juliet Packwood's delightful freckles in a manner compatible with Botticelli.

"And you were paid the seven guineas?" Holmes inquired, still inspecting the painting.

She hesitated. "Five. Paid and threatened."

"Threatened?" I asked.

"When I protested the reduction in my fee, Sir Johnny, not so jovial now, pointed out it was only for two sittings. That was mainly my doing. At my first sitting, I chanced to see the picture allegedly in need of restoration before the arrival of the restorer interrupted my scrutiny. As far as I could determine in that brief interval, there was nothing wrong with the canvas, nothing in need of repair that I could see. After two sessions, I began to feel rather queasy about the business. Perhaps it was Uncle Gerald who made me feel there was something not quite"—she searched for the word—"proper.

When I expressed my reluctance to continue, Genial Johnny became Lord Southbank in an instant, altering personalities from agreeable to terrifying, his tawny beard bristling with menace. He threatened my uncle, not in so many words, you understand, but his meaning was unmistakable. Were I ever to divulge a word of my involvement in his 'restoration' work, I might have cause to regret it, and so on in that vein. A denunciation from such a man might well prove ruinous to Uncle Gerald's small enterprise. Rather a carrot and stick approach," she concluded in a subdued voice.

"You were afraid to speak out." It was Holmes who broke the silence.

"My word against that of Sir Jonathan Van Dam, Lord Southbank? I was a coward." The young woman literally hung her head. It was the only time I had ever seen Juliet Packwood ill at ease.

"A dangerous man, as you said," I reminded her.

Sherlock Holmes concurred, "Sometimes the difference between friend and fiend is no more than the letter *r*," before adding, "but surely Lord Southbank ran the risk that someone might recognize you in the picture."

She took a deep breath and shrugged. "The chances were slight and it could always be ascribed to coincidence. How many times have people remarked on the resemblance between subjects in old paintings and those now alive. 'Why he looks just like my uncle Albert!' And so forth."

Holmes drew closer to the picture. "The painting of your face looks remarkably of a piece with the rest of the work," he observed.

"As it should. I believe when we first met I told you that Rupert Milestone was an astonishing quick-change artist with technique at his fingertips."

It foolishly struck me then that the difference between varnish and vanish was likewise an *r*.

"So you did. Miss Packwood, I must be certain I understand you. Are you telling us it was Rupert Milestone who painted this face?" He gestured to the Botticelli. "Your face?"

"It was."

"And you glimpsed the painting before its 'restoration'?"

"Only once, as I said."

"And the face . . . ?"

She hesitated. "It is hardly for me to say, Mr. Holmes."

"Your modesty becomes you, Miss Packwood."

"What was he like, Milestone?" I asked, the ache in my chest returning.

She flexed her interlaced fingers. "Wonderfully attractive, if you care for that type." My ache increased. "Leonine head, determined chin, and all that sort of thing, altogether compelling."

"Charming?" This from Holmes who cast a sidelong glance in my direction.

"I suppose . . ." she conceded absently, "but—"

"But what?" I spoke more forcefully than I intended and Holmes eyed me darkly, as much as to say, *Don't badger the witness.*

"You encountered him only twice?"

"Only twice." Another thought now occurred to her. "Now I recollect, Mr. Milestone did not strike me as particularly happy."

"Not happy? In what way? Did you converse?"

"Only when he asked me to adjust the angle of my head. Things like that. At first I thought his air of abstraction was the result of concentration, but as time went on—and believe me, time does go on when you pose—I began to sense—I'm not sure I can put it into words—to sense that far from concentrating, Milestone was in fact distracted, his mind elsewhere."

"But you did not allude to this."

"It was not my place. I was hired to pose and no more. I remember during our second session, I was on the verge of falling asleep, for sitting can be wonderfully tedious, when Sir Johnny paid a visit, to see how we were 'getting on,' as he put it."

"And was he pleased by what he saw?"

Juliet Packwood scrunched up her features as she endeavored to remember. "Pleased but annoyed at the time the work was taking. He spoke brusquely to Milestone, who endured his scolding in silence, his lips pursed with annoyance. I couldn't always see Lord Southbank because during much of the altercation he was hidden by the easel, yet it was obvious, to me at least, that there was no love lost between the two."

"Oh?" Holmes looked at me yet again. I had no difficulty recalling his having made a similar observation about Milestone and his killer.

"Though in some ways," Miss Packwood mused, "now I come to think of it, the resemblance between them was striking."

"How do you mean?" asked the detective, alert for the telling detail.

"Each cut a dandified figure, rather like two cockerels—and roosters do not get on, as I'm sure those who set them to fighting for money are perfectly aware. 'You demand too much,' Milestone fumed when Southbank had finished his haranguing. 'Do you want speed or perfection? You cannot have both.' 'I can have what I want,' the other snarled, whereupon he stormed out, leaving a heavy silence in his wake."

Holmes absorbed this intelligence before asking, "Where did this exchange take place?"

"You said that Lord Southbank's 'preservation' facility was not on the premises," I remembered.

"So I did, doctor." She spoke to me but looked only at Sherlock Holmes.

"And so you sat for your picture at 12 Cheyne Walk, in Chelsea."

It was now our guide's turn to be astonished. "How do you come to know that, Mr. Holmes?"

"It is my business to know things, Miss Packwood. When the 'restoration' was complete, Signor Garibaldi would then certify the work as authentic and after the picture was sold would doubtless receive a bonus from Sir Johnny. More carrot than stick this time, or I am much mistaken."

"I have no way of knowing, I'm sure," was the best Juliet Packwood could manage but I could see she was impressed by my companion.

We were silent now as we continued to contemplate the voluptuous Renaissance masterpiece with Juliet Packwood's face, looking as though it had always been there.

"I have known some actors in my time," Holmes began in a ruminative voice. "Without a role to play, they appear to have no personalities or traits to call their own. It is only when given a part in which to immerse themselves that they come to life."

"You have described Rupert Milestone's gift and his curse, Mr. Holmes. He could imitate with conviction and capture with ease the essence of another man's style, but from what I've seen of his own work, it was harder for Milestone to express himself in his own person."

"'The poor man's Sargent,'" I remembered.

We stood silent before the picture, contemplating what Miss Packwood had brought us to see.

"The man had everything but originality," she concurred.

"And how we prize originality," murmured Sherlock Holmes.

Our guide consulted the watch pinned to her breast. "I must return to Packwood's to help close up," she said. Still without looking at me, she strode off, leaving the detective and myself awash in new data.

9

PENTIMENTO

We returned to Baker Street exchanging only monosyllables. Our docent had given us much to think about. Whereas Sherlock Holmes's thoughts focused on what we had learned, my own ran on a separate, more troubling, track. Exhausted by the long day, I made directly for my bed, not bothering to undress, but lay disconsolately on the coverlet, staring at the darkened ceiling. Presently the fumes of formaldehyde again permeated the air.

"Watson!" the detective cried in excitement. "Come here! I want you!"

Unable to sleep in any event, I joined him. "What is it? Really, Holmes—"

"Observe, my dear fellow," he exclaimed. "Observe!"

I observed, blinking fatigue from my eyes, as the detective dipped his brush into a pool of aquamarine he had squeezed from one of the paint tubes onto his palette.

"First, I dip my brush into this lovely blue—"

"That fact has not escaped me," I responded, suppressing a yawn.

He chose to ignore my sarcasm. "Now I dip the brush with its colour, first into my supply of formaldehyde—"

"You are embalming your painting?"

"Closer than you think, my boy. Keep watching! After the formaldehyde, I dip the brush into my phenol solution, stirring the concoction of paint, formaldehyde, and phenol gently before I apply it to my dry gesso surface."

I watched as he suited action to the word.

"And then . . ?" I prompted.

He freed the canvas from its clamp and thrust it under my nose.

"And then—abracadabra!—the paint quickly dries hard as granite. Outside and in. See for yourself."

These words finally did have the effect of rousing me from my torpor and self-pity. I took the canvas and set it on the deal table. As I did so, the detective obligingly handed me his magnifier and another hatpin. (It occurred to me Mrs. Hudson must have about run out by now.)

"By Jove, Holmes!"

"Phenol and formaldehyde." He was smirking from ear to ear like a top boy. "Rupert Milestone has found a way to fool the experts. Though there is one drawback," he added.

"The artist cannot afford a mistake."

"Very good, Watson. Once the paint has hardened, no alteration is possible. No changes of any kind. But I suspect that doubt never crossed Rupert Milestone's mind. He was absolutely confident in his unique ability."

I stared at the aquamarine brushstroke. "But what was the point? As we've noted, the buyer has surely been informed by Van Dam's that the picture he contemplates acquiring has been, let us say, 'conserved.' Sir Johnny doesn't wish to be accused of such a thing as forgery."

"You surpass yourself, Watson. But where does restoration end and forgery begin? Surely it's a fine line. Certainly not a line that can be detected, let alone determined, by the ordinary viewer."

"Come to that, what is the difference between a forgery and a mere copy?" I found myself wondering.

"Excellent again!" In the gathering dark, the detective's eyes shone like beacons. "I will tell you: what separates a copy from a forgery is *something that cannot be seen!*"

"How can such a thing be possible? What is it that cannot be—?"

"*The intention*, Watson, the *intention*!" The detective was in full flow now, his mind racing as he ran through the implications. "A copy makes no attempt to deceive, it announces its reality—typically with a label—but a forgery is deception incarnate, its sole purpose to convince one and all that the false is true!"

"You put it very plainly."

"Put it more plainly still. Put the case that two paintings are placed side by side. They are identical. Put the case there is no technique or technology by which one can be distinguished from the other."

"I take it this is a hypothetical example."

"Be that as it may, my dear fellow. Very well, these two paintings cannot by any means be distinguished from one another. Yet one was painted by Leonardo da Vinci and the other by my humble self." His unblinking eyes regarded me without expression. "What makes one painting more valuable than the other?"

"Surely there is some means by which the two pictures can be—" The detective stopped me with a static, upraised forefinger.

"This is hypothetical, Watson! *The two pictures cannot be distinguished by any means!* Why then—or how, if you prefer—is one worth more than the other?"

I sighed. "I cannot imagine."

"Neither can I," Holmes surprised me by saying, "but there is this: while we may never know which was the original, it is nonetheless indisputable that *one picture could not have existed without the other.*"

He regarded me in silence as I absorbed this paradox.

"That is a most intriguing answer," I was forced to acknowledge. "But if you cannot tell which came first—"

"It is a vexing issue, we must own, but we are once more forced to acknowledge the premium we place on originality. The first man who said a woman's lips were like a rose might well lay claim to genius, but who remembers the second? Who remembers the second inventor of calculus?"*

"But if you can't tell which man said it first—"

"Regardless, Watson, forgery makes a mockery of the effort. It is originality we long to celebrate and—"

We were interrupted by the sound of the bell downstairs, followed shortly afterward by a knock on the door. "A Miss Packwood to see you, Mr. Holmes."

---

* Actually considered a tie between Newton and Leibniz.

My heart leapt at this news. My first thought was that Juliet Packwood had thought the matter over and come to speak with me, but I was quickly disabused of this notion.

"Perfect timing, Mrs. Hudson." The detective clapped his hands. "Show her in, if you please."

This was a disagreeable surprise. Aware I was not looking my best, I ran a hand through my hair and sought to fasten my collar. There was no time to do more before Juliet Packwood stepped through our door.

"I received your message, Mr. Holmes."

"Thank you for responding to it, Miss Packwood."

All I could do was gaze stupidly at the two of them, aware of a swelling discomfort in my breast. Had Holmes finally taken an interest in a woman, a woman, moreover, whom I regarded—without the least justification—as being somehow mine? And had she, to add to my woes, taken a reciprocal interest in the detective? It was clear from our last meeting that he had made a favorable impression on her.

"Would you care for tea?" Holmes asked in his most solicitous manner.

"No thank you. It is very late. Please tell me why you have asked me to come." This curt reply mollified the ache in my chest. Juliet Packwood, still choosing to ignore me, was all business.

If Holmes was disturbed by this, he gave no sign. "I would like your opinion regarding two pictures," he began, gently leading her by the elbow to the canvases we'd taken from Rupert Milestone's studio. He brought her first before the reclining nude that had so appalled me when I first beheld it. On repeated viewings, I was still shocked, but confess the beauty of the image had now pulled even with and begun to eclipse my initial outrage. With the passage of yet more time, would familiarity breed affection in place of fury? Had Holmes been right (yet again) when he suggested that artists were frequently ahead of the rest of us? Now it was no longer the painting that distressed me so much as the sight of Juliet Packwood dispassionately drawing near to examine it.

"This is interesting," was her comment.

"In what way?" asked Holmes, reaching for his pipe.

"This painting is an homage of sorts to a picture by Edouard Manet titled, *Olympia*. It hangs in Paris in the Jeu de Paume."*

"An homage, a copy, or a forgery?" He struck a match.

"Forgery?" She frowned, examining the picture once more. "An homage, without question."

"Not a copy nor a forgery, but an homage? How can you distinguish?" The familiar smell of shag I found oddly comforting. It signified my remarkable friend at work.

Juliet Packwood continued to study the picture as though to confirm her reasoning. "Though the execution is flawless, certain details have been changed."

"Changed?"

"Changed deliberately. The original is well-known, if not notorious. Deviations from its familiarity can only be understood as intentionally meant to distinguish this image from its source of inspiration."

---

*   Today *Olympia* hangs in the Musée d'Orsay.

"Can you be specific?"

She pointed. "The eyes here are a brilliant blue, but in the original they are black. Also the colour of the hair is not the same as in the original Manet, though it appears the painter in this regard has engaged in pentimento."

"Pentimento?" asked Sherlock Holmes. Pipe smoke now filled the air.

"Changed his mind. Literally, 'repented' of his earlier choice. The hair was originally another colour and since altered to the dark hue now shown here. These changes make the picture what the French term, *à la manière de*. 'In the manner of.' There is no intent here to create either a straightforward copy or forgery. Rather, a picture such as this is a willful variation on the original, and, as such may constitute a sort of private joke."

"Or private communication," Holmes ventured.

"Possibly. Joke,* communication, or commentary. Painters throughout time have indulged in secret messages. It is possible the changes here from the Manet are meant to convey such a secret."

Holmes threw me a self-satisfied glance. "As I suspected, Watson, when we first unfurled the canvas, a picture intended for an audience of two."

"Or possibly one," I said.

"Possible or probable?" Holmes asked our tutor.

---

* One example: when Marcel Duchamp painted the Mona Lisa with a moustache.

"That I am unable to say," she responded, "but there is an additional clue. Have you noticed the small convex mirror behind the Negress and the face reflected in it?"

Holmes blinked. "I have not."

Juliet Packwood handed him back the magnifying glass. "Granted the image is quite small, but unless I am mistaken, the man faintly visible in the mirror is Rupert Milestone."

Holmes drew close and held the glass before the image before passing the magnifier to me. "What do you see, Watson?"

I squinted at the enlarged detail. "It's the same face we saw in Milestone's bedroom portrait," I had to acknowledge. "So when the nude in the foreground appears to be staring at us, the viewer . . ."

"She is in fact looking at her lover, who in turn is admiring her." Holmes spoke in the respectful tone of one who has learned something new.

"Pictures, like people, hide clues, Mr. Holmes," commented Miss Packwood. "Studying them is an art in itself. The presence of the artist in a painting, for example, is a not uncommon wink, but it rules out the possibility that this picture is either a copy or a forgery. It is sometimes a gift from the lover to the object of his affection. I might note no such mirror or reflection is to be found in Manet's original."

"Intriguing," the detective murmured and was silent for some moments, evidently turning matters over in his mind before coming to a decision.

"Let me show you another picture," he said abruptly and turned her to face the Rembrandt.

Miss Packwood drew back in surprise, much as Foggerty and Signor Garibaldi had done when first confronted by the image, then leaned forward as they did, to peer more closely, frowning at what she saw.

"No opinion, Miss Packwood?"

"May I?" she asked, indicating she wished to remove the picture from the wall.

"By all means."

She gently untacked the canvas and carried it closer to the light.

"You will note the paint is hard," the detective advised her.

"Yes, but there is no varnish."

"Possibly it has been removed," I said, desperate to insert myself into the conversation.

"Were that the case, we would inevitably see traces," she responded, without looking up as she squinted through the magnifying glass. "I see no evidence of varnish."

"So, in that regard, we might characterize the picture as unfinished?" Holmes asked.

"You might."

"What about the canvas itself?"

She turned the picture over and traced a finger on the backing.

"The canvas is definitely old, both the recto and verso indicate as much."

"Possibly sixteenth or seventeenth century?"

"Possibly."

"Is it genuine?" I repeated the question I had put to Signor Garibaldi.

Juliet Packwood finally looked at me.

"It is impossible to say."

"Why is that?" inquired Holmes.

"Because in either case, the picture remains incomplete. Either Rembrandt did not apply the varnish himself and the picture languished in this state, or it was the forger who has not yet applied the varnish. Either way, this paint has never been sealed."

"But surely, without the varnish preservative, after several hundred years, these colours would no longer be as vivid?"

"Not necessarily, if the canvas was stored safely and away from sunlight. This *might* be a genuine Rembrandt, or it might be the work of a pupil or someone in his studio,"—she appeared transfixed by the image and its latent possibilities—"it is certainly *good enough* to be a Rembrandt—"

"But," said Sherlock Holmes.

Miss Packwood straightened upright and spoke briskly. "But it also might be the work of a master forger, one with unsurpassed technique, capable of mixing his own colours in the original old Dutch fashion and somehow ensuring the paint has dried solid throughout, though I can't imagine how that was managed, unless the forgery is as old as Rembrandt himself." She shrugged. "All three must remain possibilities."

"If varnish were present, would that have provided a clue?" I asked.

Our expert touched a finger to her lips, evidently giving my question some thought before answering. "Forgers are . . . artful," she finally replied. "They know that buyers looking for authenticity will inspect a canvas such as this for craquelure—"

"Those tiny fissures in the varnish that suggest age," Holmes reminded me.

She looked up from the picture. "I see you are well-informed, Mr. Holmes. Yes, your clever forger will take his finished canvas, when the varnish is dry and stiff, and roll it around something—"

"Roll it—?"

"Roll the painting around something concave—a rolling pin might do the trick. Rolling will create cracks in the varnish—the reassuring craquelure the buyer wants to see that helps suggest age. If the faker is additionally creative, he may go to the trouble of rubbing dirt into the cracks and even adding smoke from a kerosene lamp."

We contemplated this in silence, all three now scrutinizing the image and wondering just what it was we were seeing.

"Malefactors in art prove just as ingenious as those in commerce," Holmes observed.

"Art *is* commerce," our expert declared with an air of finality. "Gentlemen, I'm sorry I cannot be more helpful."

"On the contrary, Miss Packwood, you have proved invaluable. Wouldn't you agree, Watson?"

"Beyond question."

"In which case I will go," said Juliet Packwood. "If I can find a cab, I may just manage to catch the seven-fifteen at St. Pancras in time to attend my meeting."

"Meeting?"

Juliet Packwood hesitated, then squared her shoulders. "Votes for women," she explained, leaving a silence in which she evidently anticipated a challenge either from the detective or myself.

Sherlock Holmes's response startled both of us. "Before you go, Miss Packwood, I must ask you to tell us what took place between you and Lord Southbank in his restoration workshop after he ordered Rupert Milestone to leave the room."

The lady paled and groped for the back of the horsehair settee. "How did you know Lord Southbank directed anyone to leave the room?"

Holmes passed a hand over his mouth as if deliberating what he ought to say next. "Miss Packwood, in my business I have learned to listen not only to what is said and how it is said, but also to pay strict attention to what is left *un*said, a faculty I cultivated from a time I spent in Vienna. You are evidently a young woman of spirit and yet you have recently referred to yourself as a coward."

Juliet looked at me briefly. "I am a coward," she repeated quietly.

"I suspect you are being unduly hard on yourself," said Holmes. "I am trying to ascertain precisely what it is that causes you to judge yourself so harshly, and the circumstances that drove you to that unforgiving description. I cannot imagine that the woman who manifests a desire that women have the vote is easily cowed."

"If we had it—" she began, then shook her head and fell silent.

In that silence, Holmes studied the young woman—as did I, my heart racing. What was it she could not bring herself to say? "Would you prefer I leave the room?" I offered.

"No," she answered at once. I prefer you to remain."

Again, silence descended. At length Holmes spoke once more, lowering his voice to match hers. "After Rupert Milestone was out of earshot, Lord Southbank did more than threaten, did he not?"

Again Juliet flicked her eyes briefly in my direction. "He did," she conceded in a choked voice now so low as to be almost inaudible. She wiped her cheek with the back of one hand. "Afterward, I tried to pretend it did not happen," she whispered.

Holmes laid a soothing hand on her arm. "You need not tell us the rest," he assured her.

She stole a third glance in my direction before facing the detective. "What could I do, Mr. Holmes? Lord Southbank is renowned and prosperous. It would have been my word against his and I am only a woman. That is my misfortune and my shame. I must go," she repeated, looking aimlessly about but seemingly unable to release her hold on the chair.

I came forward and gently unhooked her grip. "Come. I'll help you flag a cab," I said gently.

She did not object to this and I avoided looking Holmes in the eye as we left. It was not difficult to find a hansom and Miss Packwood lodged no complaint when I climbed into the seat beside her. We sat in silence as the driver snapped the reins and we began the journey. There was no sound save the hoofbeats of our nag. After what I had heard, I was at a loss what to say or even whether I ought to break the silence.

"I must tell you—" I finally began, even as she said, "Please understand—"

"I'm sorry, please—" I interrupted.

"No, you." She bit her lip in the fashion I had seen before, then evidently changed her mind.

"You neglected to mention your DSC," she said in an unsteady voice.

"My—? Oh. Well—"

"I checked the Army Lists, as you suggested. There was your Distinguished Service Cross, plain as day. You were too modest to call it to my attention."

I understood she had no desire to return to the subject of Lord Southbank's outrage and decided to honor her wish, shaking my head and returning instead to the slaughter at Maiwand. "My medal should have gone to Murray, but he died of typhus."

"Murray?"

"My orderly. It was he who slung me over his shoulder and dragged me to safety after I was hit. When you wouldn't look at me today—"

"I was embarrassed," she said. "Now I understand a bit more about all this, I find your conduct—"

"Less reprehensible?"

This evoked a short laugh. "You mustn't put words in my mouth. Oh, very well. Less reprehensible."

I could scarcely breathe. "Then . . . we are friends once more?"

She looked at me. "We are."

I took care to exhale slowly. "Miss Packwood—"

"Since we are now to be friends, I think you might address me by my Christian name—"

"Juliet," I swallowed with difficulty. "I have tickets to the theatre on Thursday."

A small version of her smile returned. "What a fast worker you are, doctor."

"As a surgeon and former soldier, one learns that preparation is everything. Would you care to accompany me to the play?"

A silence in the dark followed and I realized I was holding my breath.

"I would." In the lamplight as we passed, I could see her smile was back.

The next half hour passed in a dream. Enclosed in this intimate space, if we conversed I have no memory of what was said. We reached St. Pancras and she alighted, saying, "No, keep the cab, doctor. Mr. Holmes will doubtless want you."

"Miss Pack—Juliet—I cannot begin to tell you—but if I'm to address you as Juliet, you must call me—"

"I can't possibly call you John," she laughed and gestured to the throng of travelers. "A dozen nearby gentlemen would respond if they heard me. How does Hamish translate from Scots Gaelic into English?"

"James."

"Very well, James it is."*

And she was gone. I remained in the cab watching her trim figure disappear into the station before rapping on the roof.

"Baker Street."

---

* This would seem at long last to clear up an issue that has long befuddled scholars; why does Watson's wife (or wives) refer to him as James rather than John? It was Dorothy Sayers who proposed the solution to this riddle. Hamish in English is James, evidently more agreeable to Juliet than the unwieldy Scottish mouthful, Hamish.

On our way, my imagination could not help but replay Juliet Packwood's unspeakable encounter with Sir Jonathan Van Dam after he had ordered Rupert Milestone from his workstation. My hands clenched tightly and my blood boiled at the thought of what had happened next and what I would do to the scoundrel were I ever to confront him, but these vengeful thoughts mercifully gave way to more agreeable ones. Juliet and I were once more friends. And who knows where matters might go from there?

Even without my state of intoxication, I could not have imagined what awaited me the following morning.

10

SUSPECTS

I could not sleep, so transported was I by the prospect of a rosy future with Juliet Packwood. I was building castles in Spain (or Fulham, at any rate), in which we would share our bliss-filled lives. So far had my cart outrun any horse that I gave little thought to Holmes and what such an alteration in our domestic arrangements might bring. I confess I was little troubled on that score and in my fancy, the detective was relegated to an obliging background role. "So pleased for you, old man," was as far as I got. And, now that I thought of it, as I struggled for sleep, all I was likely to get. Holmes was not a demonstrative creature. Whatever his feelings about my second defection, he was unlikely to reveal them.*

---

* Of his original marriage, Holmes referred to it as "the only time the good Watson deserted me."

The possibility of a second marriage (my cart, so speedy by this time, had left its horse in the barn), caused me some confused thoughts with regard to my beloved Mary. Someone has maintained that happily married folk invariably remarry after the loss of a mate, if only to recapture the happiness they associate with wedlock. How would I feel, if following my death (were such a thing possible), I were to somehow learn in the spirit world that my wife planned to remarry? This prospect caused my living self a twinge, but would I expect my wife to mourn me like the Widow of Windsor, forever draped in black, following the death of the Prince Consort? Victoria Regina and Juliet Watson? I had to smile at the thought. Certainly not. Life must be lived! This much I understood after Maiwand and my chance meeting with Sherlock Holmes. I would devote my life to Juliet's happiness. I would make up for the awfulness she had endured at the hands of that monster. And if my death were to precede hers (by now, as I punched my pillow yet again, we were man and wife), would I not hope for her to find happiness elsewhere? The answer was bittersweet but inevitable. One is either living or merely paying rent.

It must have been well after three when, after tossing and turning my bedding into a tangled heap that resembled nothing so much as the Gordian knot, I finally managed to fall into a slumber so profound I might as well have swallowed opium. When I was awakened the following morning by a loud thumping, I first supposed it was the beating of my heart, before I was able to make out the muffled voice of Mrs. Hudson calling for Holmes.

Pulling back the curtains, I fumbled for my watch, astonished to see it was after eleven. I threw on my robe and stepped squinting into our sitting room, flummoxed to find Inspector Lestrade seated opposite the detective who had evidently just finished his breakfast and perusal of the morning papers.

"Both dead?" he was saying, setting down his copy of *The Globe*.

"Afraid so, Mr. Holmes."

"Who has died?" I asked, reaching eagerly for the last of the tea, which was now stone cold.

"Good morning, doctor," said the ferret-like policeman. "Yes, I was just explaining to Mr. Holmes that a Signor Garibaldi and his housekeeper in Chelsea were found dead early this morning by Constable Higgins on his rounds."

So astounded was I by this news that all I could do was open and close my mouth like a fish.

"Pray be precise as to details," Holmes instructed, waving me into a chair and closing his eyes as was his custom when listening to the particulars of a case. But despite the assumption of his professional demeanor, I could see this development had rattled him.

"Well, sir, according to constable Higgins, he was on Cheyne Walk, following his usual beat, when he detected the faint odor of gas which grew stronger as he neared number twelve."

"The time being?" asked Holmes.

"The time . . ." Lestrade consulted his notes. "The time was just before eight this morning. Higgins inspected the premises and discovered the door bolted and the mullioned windows front and side securely fastened—but there was no mistaking the prevalence of the smell. He smashed one window, enabling him to confirm the source of the odor, but it was too small for anyone to fit. He thereupon notified his superiors and was soon joined by ten additional constables. Unable to force the sturdy bolt on the door and sharing Higgins's alarm, they walked 'round the premises and discovered the glass conservatory which looks to have been erected over what was once a small garden. There was a glass door with a brass escutcheon, but as time was of the essence, rather than wrestle with another lock, they chose simply to shatter one of the adjacent panes with a truncheon, whereupon, instantly overpowered by fumes, they were obliged to step back and cover their noses with wet kerchiefs in order to step over the shards and enter."

The policeman paused as if the choking fumes he described had caused him to run out of breath.

"Continue, Lestrade."

"They immediately detected the hiss from the jet in the corridor and threw open every window, but it was too late. Signor Garibaldi and his housekeeper—"

"Leopoldina," Holmes remembered, his eyes still closed.

"You know her name?" the inspector cast a shrewd look in the detective's direction.

Holmes smiled without opening his eyes. "As you doubtless saw the visiting card I left on Signor Garibaldi's worktable, you surely know, Inspector, that Dr. Watson and I were at number 12 last night, hence your visit today."

"So we did, Mr. Holmes. The card had been torn to shreds, but I managed to piece it together." This was said with a distinct note of pride. "Yes. Both were asphyxiated. The night before was chilly you will recall and it appears the windows had been closed on that account. But when the lights were extinguished, one jet was inexplicably left open."

"The one in the downstairs corridor."

"Just so," the inspector flipped a page in his book, "the one in the corridor."

"And the bodies?"

"Both were quite blue by the time they were found." He shook his head. "I understand Signor Gari—" he consulted his notes.

"—baldi," I said, slurping the last of the tea and struggling to gather my wits about me.

"Just so," the little man repeated. "I understand this Garibaldi was celebrated or at any rate well-regarded in his profession? Something to do with art?"

"That is my understanding," agreed Holmes solemnly.

The inspector chose not to pursue this line of inquiry. "Apparently a dreadful accident," he concluded.

I looked to see what Holmes made of this theory. Instead of answering, he took his time, packing, lighting, and puffing on his trusty cherrywood.

"Inspector, may I pose a few questions of my own?" he asked as the reassuring aroma rose from the bowl.

"By all means, sir."

"What was the position of the bodies when they were found? Were they in their beds?"

"They were, sir. As you doubtless noted, the house, dating from that era, is quite small, so it didn't take long for the gas to do its work. The maidservant was in her garret quarters and Signor—the art expert—was sitting upright in his room situated on the ground floor near his workplace. It seems his—"

"Skeletal structure," I interjected.

"Just so, doctor. His skeletal structure required that he sleep in a sitting posture. And also discouraged his use of stairs, hence the location of his room."

Holmes said nothing.

"Anything else, sir?" The man was as anxious as if he were sitting for his examinations.

The detective puffed placidly on his pipe before speaking. "Do you know how long Signor Garibaldi and his servant had lived at 12 Cheyne Walk?"

"One moment—" Lestrade broke off his answer to consult his notebook. "I believe he'd leased the place for over five years."

"That is suggestive, wouldn't you say, Watson?" The detective glanced at me meaningfully.

"Indubitably," I replied, having not the least notion what he was getting at.

"One final question, Lestrade. You say the front door could not be opened?"

The man smoothed his moustache with a chubby forefinger. "We gave it up as a bad job, sir. Those old houses with their thick doors and almost medieval bolts. A man's home is his castle and all that. Might as well use a battering ram as they did in the old days. It was less time-consuming to simply smash a conservatory glass at the rear. Air out the place faster, as well, come to that."

"Most helpful," murmured the detective.

Inspector Lestrade now cleared his throat, seemingly preparing himself for a change of subject. "May I ask, sir, why you had gone to see, Signor, uh, Gari—?"

"—baldi" supplied the detective. "I wished to consult him on a technical matter related to his field."

"Art?"

My companion hesitated. "Yes, art."

"May I ask," the other gently pressed, "whether this matter of art was connected to the recent death of the artist, Rupert Milestone?"

Again, Holmes hesitated. "In a way. It pertained to questions of technique, specifically as related to a client of mine, whose identity I am not at liberty to disclose."

"Mr. Holmes," Lestrade cleared his throat once more, both men ill at ease now, "I respectfully remind you that I am currently investigating two suspicious deaths."

"Which you have even now characterized as an accident, Inspector."

The policeman cleared his throat and stroked his moustache a third time. "Be that as it may, sir, may I ask, at what time would you estimate you and Dr. Watson left Signor Gari-balding and his housekeeper?"

Holmes shot me a look.

"Close to five, as I recall," I said.

With his notebook propped on one knee, Lestrade, with a look of fierce concentration, licked the tip of his pencil and carefully jotted our answers on a fresh page. I confess the sight of the book as these entries were added caused me some unease.

"It would appear," the policeman said, without looking up, "that you and Dr. Watson were the last people to see Signor Garibalding and his housekeeper alive."

This remark further unsettled me. I took it to imply Holmes and I were under a cloud of suspicion. This was not a role usually allotted the detective and myself.

"Appearances can be deceptive," said Holmes mildly.

There followed a lengthy silence after which the small man, understanding Holmes was not about to volunteer anything further, sighed and rose.

"Thank you, Mr. Holmes."

"You are most welcome, Inspector Lestrade."

At the door, the policeman turned to face us. "You will contact us if you recollect anything that might bear on our investigation, Mr. Holmes."

"You may rely on it, Inspector Lestrade. And please convey my greetings to Inspector Gregson."

Nettled by this Parthian shot, Lestrade made a face and left, shutting the door behind him.

When out of hearing, Holmes permitted himself a sigh of his own, setting aside his pipe and dabbing at his brow with a breakfast napkin.

"*Terra incognita*, Watson."

"Holmes this is absurd. You know we had nothing to do with the deaths of these two unfortunate people."

"I am not entirely certain that is the case." Holmes knocked the bowl of his pipe too vigorously against the ashtray, discharging a shower of glowing embers over the rug before extinguishing them with the toe of his Persian slipper.

"What are you saying? When we left the house the gas was lit and both those people were very much alive. Had the jet in the corridor remained unlit while other lights burned, the place would shortly have exploded and likely damaged houses in the vicinity as well."

"Oh, as to that there can be no doubt. We certainly had no motive to harm the man or his servant. I meant indirectly responsible. And I was referring to myself, not you, my boy. It was a great mistake to have revealed my identity to Signor Garibaldi. I very much fear that stroke of vanity on my part led to the demise of the man and his unfortunate housekeeper."

I could see this idea weighed heavily on my friend and determined to stamp out this notion before it took root.

"How on earth do you reach such a conclusion? Garibaldi was forever restricted by his impairment. Is it not possible, that, tiring of his debilitating circumstances, he chose to end his life?"

"Suicide?" The detective considered this before shaking his head. "Out of the blue? And was he comfortable with the idea of dispatching his faithful maidservant, as well? I think it unlikely. What I find more plausible is that I frightened the man. My questions, let alone my identity, placed him on alert. So much so that after we left, he tore my card to pieces, as enraged monarchs of old slew messengers bearing ill tidings. As I implied to his face, Signor Garibaldi was involved in Lord Southbank's swindle, certifying the authenticity of some of Van Dam's questionable old master inventory. You will recall I asked if he received a commission on each painting to which he attached his imprimatur. I am wondering if the poor man, alarmed by my inquiries, made the mistake of warning Lord Southbank—"

"Wherever the rogue has got to," I struck in. "I swear if I ever meet that villain I will not be held accountable for my actions."

"I share your indignation, Watson, but our immediate problem demands precedence. If he could not reach Sir Johnny, perhaps Signor Garibaldi managed to contact someone in his employ, to whom he communicated his fear that the bamboozle was up. Or soon likely to be."

It was not often that I was able to poke holes in the detective's chain of reasoning, but here I could not resist. "And in the space of that short time, this hypothetical someone was alerted, managed to travel to and enter Signor Garibaldi's locked home, turn on the gas, and asphyxiate him and his housekeeper? And leave the house still locked? Holmes, that is impossible."

"As impossible as Houdini walking through a brick wall. Which we've allowed cannot be done."

"Holmes, you are the apostle of logic," I insisted. "How could such a person have been notified? Even telegrams are not that fast."

"You seem to have forgotten one detail, Watson."

"And what might that be?"

"The telephone on Signor Garibaldi's worktable."

That fact had indeed escaped my attention.

"Ah, yes. So I had. You think in his excitement he telephoned someone?"

The detective rose to his feet. "I think we had best ascertain for ourselves."

"Ascertain what? I'm not following you."

"Ascertain whether the police, in their understandable haste, ever troubled to examine the door they scorned to unlock at the back of the conservatory."

⌇

"Doolittle, is it?" Holmes inquired of the helmeted policeman when we presented ourselves an hour later at 12 Cheyne Walk. "How's the missus? I see you've added another future constable to your brood."

The man smiled broadly. "And how did you come to know that, sir? Little Lionel made his appearance only last week."

The detective pointed. "You are not yourself a smoker, as I recall, Doolittle, yet your breast pocket is bulging with cigars."

This brought forth a hearty laugh. "So true, Mr. 'olmes, would you care to join the celebration? These may be a bit stale by now."

"Another time, Doolittle." Holmes gestured to the door. "Is it possible for us to inspect the premises?"

Passersby at this midday hour were few, nannies pushing perambulators and an elderly gentleman escorting his dog, who stopped to sniff questioningly at the last of the odors at number 12 before his owner was waved on.

"Sorry, Mr. 'olmes, no one is allowed inside at present," said the affable policeman. "Inspector Gregson is still searching for clues."

"Ah," replied Holmes, maintaining a straight face, "then it wouldn't do to disturb him. Would you have any objection if we walked 'round to look at the conservatory?"

The man frowned as he considered the request. "I suppose that's all right," he declared, his countenance clearing, "seeing as it's you, sir. But no going inside, mind. There's another man posted at the rear."

"That is understood. Many thanks, Doolittle, and again, my congratulations. Come along, Watson."

We followed the outer wall of the house to where the brick adjoined the modern glass addition. As we'd been told, another sentinel stood by the shattered pane of glass through which his brethren had gained entry. The smell of gas had by now entirely dissipated.

"No fear, constable, we've no intention of breaching the precincts," Holmes assured the man.

"Very good, sir. But I'll keep an eye, if it's all the same."

"Please do. I understand that rather than wasting time on another locked door, the police employed the simple expedient of breaking a glass pane to gain entry?"

"I couldn't say, sir. I wasn't here this morning."

"I trust you've no objection were I to examine this broken glass?"

The ruddy-faced man thought about this. "I suppose that's all right."

"But I just wonder—" Holmes reached for the brass knob of the conservatory door and twisted it.

"Sir, I must ask you not to—"

As we watched in astonishment, Holmes gently pulled open the door. "*Mirabile dictu*," he remarked, "what have we here?"

"Unlocked!" I exclaimed.

"Eliminate the impossible," Holmes murmured, as much to himself as me. "Had they tried the knob, the police might have saved themselves the trouble of smashing the adjacent glass." He looked around. "I see no signs of a key, do you? May we look for it, constable?"

The man, surprised by the revelation of the unlocked door, offered no objection. A brief search on the grounds and the nearby bushes failed to reveal a key.

"That I would call suggestive," said Sherlock Holmes.

"The missing key?"

"All of it, Watson. All of it. We'll be on our way," said he addressing the policeman. "You will inform Inspector Gregson of this development?"

"I will, Mr. Holmes."

Upon our return to Baker Street, I saw Holmes gather his usual assortment of pillows and bolsters, methodically arranging them on the rug in his accustomed nest-like configuration before donning his mouse-coloured dressing gown.

"A three-pipe problem?"

"At the very least, Watson." Holmes squatted at the center of his creation, lighting pipe number one and looking for all the world like Alice's caterpillar.

"May I open a window?"

He nodded solemnly.

"You believe last night was no mischance?"

He blew a plume of thoughtful smoke. "I do."

"Murder, then?"

"Murder most foul, Watson."

"And do you know the identity of the murderer?"

The caterpillar puffed in silence for some moments, closing his eyes as if surrendering to a trance. "Pending one additional piece of information, I believe I do."

I knew there was no point in asking anything more.

11

THE THING

It had been some time since I had donned evening dress and there was no question my trousers fit more snugly than the last time I had occasion to wear them. Mindful of the evening's importance, I took my time, vigorously brushing the dark clothes and holding them to the window, inspecting them for lint or moth activity. By luck as much as anything else, what I saw when I studied my reflection in the glass I judged presentable. "Especially in low light," I told myself.

When I left my room, an overcoat over my arm, once more smoothing my top hat with my elbow, Holmes was where I had left him, with closed eyes under a perfect halo of blue smoke. I tried to walk quietly but a squeaking floorboard roused him.

"Off to the theatre and supper, are you?"

"How do you know?"

"When I observe the unaccustomed formality of your attire and add to that your recent infatuation, it is not a stretch to imagine with whom you are dining and what your plans for the evening are. Besides which, if you persist in throwing your coat over your arm, your tickets to *The Importance of Being Earnest* are in danger of sliding out of their pocket before you ever arrive at the St. James Theatre.'"*

"Notwithstanding the hour, I see your powers remain undimmed."

"My dear fellow, you will give the game away. Present my compliments to Miss Packwood." His eyes closed again.

"Any progress?" I asked at the door.

"Awaiting additional data," he answered without opening them.

It was not clear whether he expected these to arrive from without or within.

When I called for her, Juliet Packwood appeared breathtaking in a gown of dark blue satin, one hand inserted in a white muff. I was astounded by the transformation. In our formal clothes, we surveyed each other almost as if we were strangers, but I was aware that at this instant, giddy with anticipation, we were as far from strangers as could be imagined. The air was charged with promise and the evening that followed unfolded like a dream—the same dream I had been living since the day we met.

The play was enchanting, nothing but gaiety and wit, though I confess that as far as I was concerned, *King Lear* would have failed to dampen our spirits. Quite without my being aware of the moment when it happened, I realized we were holding hands.

---

* Watson has apparently omitted to inform Juliet of his acquaintance with the play's author, also detailed in the case known as *The West End Horror*.

When I became aware of her fingers laced with mine, I dared not move nor laugh too heartily at the play for fear of disturbing the connection flowing between us like an electric current.

Afterward came supper at The Langham, which I have no recollection of consuming, and again what was said reached my ears only through a mist of wonder and happiness. When, after midnight, I returned her to her lodgings in Goodge Street, both of us were slightly the worse for several glasses of Veuve Clicquot.

"What a delightful evening, James. The play was so very funny. I can't remember when I've enjoyed myself as much," she said at the door, searching her reticule industriously but ineffectually for her latchkey.

"Nor I. The play was wonderful," said I.

She found the key and looked at me. "Not just the play."

Before we knew it, we had kissed.

"Someone will see," I said, breathlessly.

"Not at this hour, dearest. And no one we know."

We kissed again.

The cabbie waited in tactful silence.

"Good night, James."

"Good night." I stood rooted to the spot until I heard the lock click.

"Watson, your hat is about to fall off," said Sherlock Holmes, alerted by the same creaking floorboard as I attempted a silent entry into our darkened lodgings.

I managed to catch hold of my hat before it toppled to the floor. Clicking on the light, I beheld Holmes ensconced where I had left him, shrouded, if possible, by even more smoke.

"I take it from your schoolboy grin the evening was a success?"

"It was . . ." I broke off, coughing from all the smoke, but in any event unable, in my euphoria, to find the words.

"I see." Was it the champagne or did I detect an air of melancholy in those two words?

"Have there been any breakthroughs?" I asked in a determined effort to return to Earth.

He hesitated. "Let that keep for the time being."

His answer puzzled me. "Have you received the data you were awaiting?"

"I daresay it won't arrive until tomorrow. But when it does, I anticipate the missing piece will fill the jigsaw puzzle that has proved so vexing and the image will at last be complete. Could I interest you in some cold coffee?" He gestured to the tray Mrs. Hudson must have delivered in the interim. My first impulse was to decline and totter off to bed in my exulted state, but seeing his worn countenance caused me to change my mind. My happiness made room for generosity. I tugged off my white scarf and carefully poured the coffee into two cups, though in my semi-intoxicated state I sensed the odds were against me.

Holmes eyed my efforts with the impassivity of a Buddha.

"Have you made sense of any of this?" I asked, seating myself in the nearest chair and sipping the stale brew.

"Have *you*?" the detective countered. "Come, wake yourself up and be that luminous conductor of light for which I value you so highly. You know there's nothing so wonderfully clarifying as to listen to another's statement of the facts."

"I'll do my best," I said, unable, by this point, to suppress a yawn. The coffee was revolting but I swallowed another mouthful. "I am all attention." Holmes appeared haggard but fully alert. Hours on those cushions had not tired him in the least.

For my part, I determined to focus my best efforts on my friend's behalf. "Here is what I make of matters," I began, clearing my throat, "Lord Southbank engaged Rupert Milestone for the purposes of restoration work."

"Very good. This much is certain."

"Realizing the versatility of his hire, he expanded the painter's responsibilities. From mere cosmetic repairs, Milestone was graduated to 'improvements,' especially concerning the physiognomy of young women designed to appeal to gentlemen with a taste for such subjects."

Holmes listened, fingertips pressed together, his eyes closed, as usual. It was all I could do to keep mine open.

"Continue, old man."

I swallowed more coffee. "Old masters, as Mycroft informed you, do not grow on trees, and so it was perhaps inevitable that Sir Johnny hit upon the notion of ordering them up from scratch, or, as Miss Packwood put it—"

"Ah, yes, the well-informed and pleasant Miss Packwood," the detective teased.

"Or as Miss Packwood described it," I persisted, ignoring his gibe, "paintings 'in the manner of—'"

"*À la manière de,*" Holmes remembered the original French.

"Not precisely copies, but homemade Rembrandts, Caravaggios, and all the rest."

"Splendid, Watson."

"Initially, Milestone threw himself into the project with resolution and ingenuity. As a painter he had met with only middling success, so it is hardly surprising that the notion of fooling the experts must have appealed to a man who believed his talents were not properly appreciated."

"'The poor man's Sargent', yes."

"By his reasoning, if he could paint as well as Sargent why was he not rewarded like Sargent? He was not, because he was forbidden to sign Sargent's name. Or Rembrandt's, for that matter. To Milestone's way of thinking, that was not art, that was autographs. One may concede his point," I added.

"Very good, Watson. What else?"

"Doubtless money was an incentive for Milestone as well, for his employer kept the man on a tight lead. But for his work to withstand the scrutiny of the dreaded authenticators (those not on Sir Johnny's payroll), he knew that, at a minimum, his oils would have to pass the pin test for hardness, so he purchased a kiln to dry the insides of his handiwork. When that didn't answer, he resorted to chemistry and managed to solve the problem."

"Truly, Watson, even at this hour, you shine."

The detective's praise did what cold coffee could not. I was now fully awake and plunged ahead as the disparate pieces fell into place.

"But disagreements between them arose regarding compensation. Lord Southbank, as we have learned, is a hard bargainer. He shortchanged Miss Packwood for her services and doubtless underpaid Milestone, even as Miss Packwood overheard him demand quicker results from his harassed accomplice."

"Does that not strike you as penny-pinching in a man of Lord Southbank's means?"

"Think, my dear Holmes," I enjoyed imitating the detective's delivery. "With palatial emporia to maintain in London, Paris, New York, and elsewhere, the villain has a stupendous overhead! To uphold Van Dam's facade, he must produce and sell more old masters than he may legally be able to lay hands on. If they are real, the likelihood is they will cost him dearly. Hence his obsession with Milestone's unique gift, but even there he is obliged to cut corners and drive a hard bargain. This may also reflect his origins and instincts as a peddler of knicknacks on the streets of Brussels."

"Excellent. Continue, old man."

"Ah, but matters came to a head on the night of the blizzard when Van Dam visited the artist's studio, undoubtedly to reiterate his demand for quicker results."

"Watson, your evening with Miss Packwood seems to have done you a power of good," the detective exclaimed, causing me to rush on.

"But Rupert Milestone was not a man to be broken on Lord Southbank's wheel. As you surmised, words suddenly became blows, whereupon Milestone was slain by his enraged employer, who then lugged the body during the snowstorm in the dead of night to Kensington Gardens and, in a feat of morbid inspiration, interred it in a hastily improvised snowman before fleeing the country and counting on the weather to conceal the deed until he had made good his escape. Does that about cover it?" I asked, pleased with my summation.

"I would call it superb, Watson."

"My dear Holmes—"

"As far as it goes."

I heard these words with a sinking heart, realizing almost at once there was much in my summation left unaccounted for. "For example?" I demanded feebly.

"For example, it does not explain why Rupert Milestone, a practicing artist, had not the slightest trace of paint under his fingernails—"

"We have established the man was something of a dandy," I protested, "fastidious in dress and doubtless personal—"

"Nor have you accounted for the mysterious break-in at number 7 Turncoat Lane and the disappearance of the banknotes we so scrupulously returned to their original places of concealment."

"Ah, yes, I'd—"

"Nor yet explained how the missing razor traveled from the tawny hairs in the wash basin to the site of the struggle and the murder."

"Yes, I realize that remains—"

"And your summation, plausible as it is, does not take into account the intruder who succeeded in asphyxiating Signor Garibaldi and his unfortunate housekeeper, though we now know how the killer gained admittance to a locked home. He was somehow in possession of a key to the conservatory door."

"Possibly the door was left unlocked," I offered.

"By accident or design? I judge that suspiciously convenient, Watson, and so do you. Either the murderer was in possession of the conservatory key or a confederate arranged his entry."

"How could that possibly have been managed?"

"Think, Watson."

I cudgeled my brains and the answer came to me. "Oh, yes! Signor Garibaldi, using his telephone, made the mistake of alerting someone in Sir Johnny's employ, informing him that Sherlock Holmes was closing in on the swindle."

"Excellent, my boy."

"And the recipient of that call acted swiftly to prevent the impaired authenticator becoming a witness for the prosecution."

"You scintillate, Watson. But who? And, last but not least, what of the missing shoes on Rupert Milestone's frozen feet? What has become of them?"

"Ah, yes, I did omit the shoes."

We sat in silence while Holmes emitted yet another puff of smoke. "Curious," he murmured at length.

"What is curious?"

"I was remembering the observation I made on Portobello Road, to the effect that art cannot exist without a frame."

"Holmes, I fail to see what you are—"

"All art of any and every kind requires a frame, Watson! A frame defines the limits of the artist's effort and effect! A book—even an epic such as the *Iliad*, which would seem to encompass all life—is nonetheless limited by its covers. Those covers define the extent of the poem as a frame acknowledges the extent of what is depicted within it."

"What about plays?" I demanded, relieved to abandon discussion of the gaps in my reasoning, and thinking instead of the performance I had just attended.

My companion shrugged. "Defined by the curtain that rises and falls at the start and the finish. For a play to encompass all life, the curtain must rise and stay up. No art is able to do this. All, sooner or later, in one form or another, must exist within a frame."

I was blearily trying to follow this. "And when there is no frame?"

He heaved a sigh. "Without the frame, it isn't art; it's life."

This digression, for such I regarded it, rendered us both silent for a time, during which my mind, still at loose ends, began to wander. Suddenly, unable to contain myself, I burst into laughter.

"Watson?" The detective regarded me with an arched eyebrow.

"Forgive, my dear fellow. It's only that talking of plays, you've put me in mind of Lady Bracknell—"

"Who?"

"From the play tonight. I confess I don't remember much, but Lady Bracknell says the cleverest things. When she asks her daughter's suitor, 'Do you smoke, Mr. Worthing?' and he admits he does, she responds, 'Excellent. A man should have an occupation.' Don't you find that amusing?" I gestured to the detective's tobacco halo. "Especially in your case at present—"

"Watson, we are trying to reach a—"

"Oh, and another time, her nephew says, 'Poor lady so-and-so—since her husband's death, I hear her hair has turned quite gold with grief.' I thought—"

The effect of this remark was the last thing I might have anticipated. Sherlock Holmes bolted to his feet, having bitten through his pipe stem.

"*Watson!*"

"Whatever is the—"

Holmes rushed over to Milestone's pale nude and held it up before him like a herald's proclamation. "Watson, you are indeed luminous!" The detective gaped with wonderment at the canvas.

"I'm afraid I don't—"

"Pentimento, Watson. *Pentimento!*"

"I beg your pardon? Holmes it is late—"

"The painter changed his mind!"

"I still don't—"

"Bring a light, man!"

The harsh urgency in his voice was such that I obeyed at once.

Using his pen knife, the detective began delicately scraping away at the pale face of the woman depicted in the painting we had retrieved from Milestone's.

"Holmes, what are you—"

"The painter had no need to employ chemistry to harden these colours," he exclaimed. "He wasn't creating a fake, he was sending a love note."

"I still don't under—"

"Look, man!"

I did. Under his careful ministrations, slivers of paint revealed the painter's original intention on the reclining woman's left cheek.

What I saw caused me to sink into my chair.

"Dear God."

"Indeed." Holmes laid aside the penknife.

We stared at the painting.

"What will you do?"

Finally showing signs of fatigue, the detective set down the picture. "What *can* I do?"

"Inform the police, surely—"

He stretched out his arms, flexing his fingers. "Inform them of what, Watson? Rupert Milestone is deceased and by now Lord Southbank may well be in Tibet. Besides which"—he trailed off, yawning—"the picture, as I have termed it, may be complete in its frame, but not the case."

"The missing shoes and razor, the clean fingernails of the painter—"

"All of the above, Watson, and what's more, I am still awaiting the last piece of data."

"But you said you knew the identity of Milestone's killer."

"Knowing and proving are different things, Watson. We suffer a shortage of witnesses." He stretched and yawned again. "No one other than the combatants saw what happened."

"Another three-pipe problem?"

"I think I must resort to an older remedy."

I dreaded to hear these words. "I trust there is no cocaine still on the premises."

He laughed. "None, my dear fellow, I assure you. I refer merely to the realm of Morpheus. I must sleep. I don't know how you manage to fill these rooms with smoke, Watson," the detective proffered a mischievous smile, "but it is impossible for a man to think clearly amid this miasma."

Pleased with this raillery, he strode toward his room, abandoning his broken pipe in the ashtray. I shortly followed his example, retiring to my own quarters, but remained awake, my brain laying siege to my heart. It was hard to think clearly when happiness, a narcotic to rival Holmes's seven-per-cent solution, was flowing through my veins.

I must have drifted off, I've no idea how long, before my door was flung open with a crash.

"Watson!"

I started and squinted at my friend, standing on the threshold, illumined from behind.

"What's the matter?"

"The play's the thing!"

I sat up with difficulty and fumbled for the light, revealing Holmes, disheveled and unshaven, a wild look in his bloodshot eyes. In my disoriented state, I briefly wondered if I was seeing an apparition.

"Holmes, what are you talking about? What has *The Importance of Being*—"

"*Hamlet*, Watson. *Hamlet*! The play's the thing, wherein we'll catch the conscience of the king! Oh, I perceive you're asleep," he noted in a calmer voice.

"Very astute."

"Very well. Let us wait for morning." He shut the door more quietly than he'd opened it.

Waiting was easier said than done. If I'd experienced difficulty sleeping before, the detective's excited and cryptic words served to compound that difficulty. What had *Hamlet* to do with anything? I lay awake, torn between a lover's newfound exhilaration and the devouring curiosity that infused all my relations with Sherlock Holmes.

Neither of these feelings was conducive to rest.

12

THE MOUSETRAP

"**L**unacy!"

"Now, Watson—"

"This is the sort of play you had in mind? Have you taken leave of your senses?"

"Every precaution will be taken, I assure—"

"No, Holmes. It is out of the question."

"One moment, dearest." Juliet laid a hand on my arm. We were sitting in a semicircular banquette at Simpson's, debating in rising voices the detective's brainstorm, which, until this moment, I had not dreamt entailed the participation of the woman with whom I was now desperately in love. "As this involves me, I believe I must have some say."

"Involves you as a Judas goat? The notion is preposterous! I absolutely forbid it."

"May I take your order or would you like more time?" our waiter inquired.

The detective held up a hand. "More time, please, Alfred."

"James, dear," Juliet said quietly when the man had gone, "without intending to trespass on any of your masculine prerogatives, I must point out that I am my own person and must have some say in decisions that affect me. In time, as you surely know, women will have the vote—"

"We are not discussing the vote. We are talking about your life—"

"I have my cowardice to atone for," she interrupted me quietly but firmly. "Wherever he is concealing himself, I have a score to settle with Lord Southbank and this may be my chance."

Seated across from us, as my loyalties were put to the test, Holmes appeared absorbed by the menu, which we both knew from memory.

"Besides," Juliet added cheerfully, "I have every faith in the assurances given by Sherlock Holmes as I am certain you do as well."

"That is not the point," I protested.

"Then what is?" she soothed. "The final piece of the puzzle fell into the hands of Mr. Holmes this morning, as he anticipated it would. Not to make use of it—"

"I must remind you there's no limit to the malice of which the villain is capable, as you, of all people, very well know." Seeing her stricken expression, I regretted this unfortunate remark and rushed to change the subject. "The last person Lord Southbank feared might betray him was asphyxiated—along with an innocent woman." I looked past her to the detective. "Holmes, there must be an alternative to this harebrained proposal."

Holmes did not take his eyes from the menu. "If there is I should be keen to learn it," he murmured. "We ourselves are too well-known to work our scheme alone—"

"*Your* scheme," I corrected, unwilling to let him shift responsibility onto any shoulders other than his own.

"—and the Scotland Yarders would sooner break a window than trouble to twist a doorknob," he went on, ignoring my correction and following his own train of thought. "It seems to me Miss Packwood may be the strongest card in our otherwise not-very-promising hand."

"I have no difficulty following your reasoning, Mr. Holmes." To my consternation Juliet was now aligning herself with the detective.

"But should you be recognized, dearest!"

If Holmes made anything of our repeated endearments, he gave no sign.

"Why would I? There is nothing to connect us," Juliet countered. "I will make certain not to use my own name. That should minimize any possibility of identification."

"She's right, there, you must admit, my dear fellow."

"Holmes, kindly refrain from putting in your oar. I will not have Miss Packwood planted in Lauriston Gardens to lure—"

"You must own there's a certain symmetry, Watson."

"Symmetry be damned! Certain death is more like it. This discussion does not concern you, Holmes."

"Stop this, both of you. Behaving like children." This from Juliet in response to our rising voices.

Obeying, Holmes spoke more quietly. "I will be present the whole time, my dear fellow—and so will you."

Here I made the mistake of hesitating and the detective pressed his advantage. "Be reasonable, Watson. It's been fifteen years. The place is entirely different now, as is the landlord. The whole Lauriston Gardens business is long forgotten."

This exchange finally served to slow Juliet's headlong embrace of the detective's maneuverings. "What Lauriston Gardens business? Will one of you please tell me what you are talking about?"

Holmes and I exchanged glances, his expression plainly daring me to take the bull by the horns.

"It's rather a long story, dearest."

She favored me with one of her dazzling smiles. "As we've not yet ordered breakfast I don't see why I've not time to hear it." Alfred, as if on cue, drifted back in our direction. "I should like the scones and black coffee, if you please," she told him. When the man had taken the rest of our order, she sat back. "Now then, you two, let's have it all."

"The doctor is entitled to relate it," said Holmes. "It was, after all, the first of my cases which he set down for the public, albeit with a dose of lurid embellishment. *A Study in Scarlet*, indeed."*

"The title was the editor's, not mine," I grumbled, revisiting an old argument. "Be that as it may, I don't believe this is the time or place to read it." I crossed my arms to lend emphasis to my refusal.

---

*   *A Study in Scarlet, Being a Reprint from the Reminiscences of John H. Watson, M.D.*, is the first of Holmes's cases recorded by the doctor and contains the most complete account of their initial meeting.

"There at least we agree," said the detective, "but I daresay you can manage a précis, old man."

"Let us have the précis, by all means," Juliet pleaded, gently unfolding my arms.

I sighed, discovering that, like the detective, Juliet Packwood was hard to resist. "Some fifteen years ago, when this gentleman"—indicating Holmes—"and I first began sharing rooms, I first became aware of his profession as a consulting detective."

"The world's only consulting detective," Holmes amended.

"I believe you nominated me to tell the story," said I, more determined than ever to scotch this ill-conceived undertaking.

"I beg your pardon. Proceed."

"Fifteen years ago," I huffed, "this gentleman invited me to accompany him to Lauriston Gardens, a block of houses to let off the Brixton Road. A murder had taken place at Number 3 and it was there that I first witnessed his astonishing abilities. From the condition of the shabby, unfurnished rooms and of the body lying on the floor, Holmes was able to deduce a world of detail that ultimately led to the murderer's apprehension."

"Which I now propose to do again, Miss Packwood."

"A body on the floor," Juliet repeated, shaking her head as if to clear it. "And you now propose—"

"He now proposes tethering you as bait in those same precincts!" My voice rose once more.

Wide-eyed, Juliet turned to the detective. "Is this true?"

"Your coffee," said Alfred, now pouring the brew smoothly into our cups. A leaden silence ensued as this ritual was completed.

"To an extent," Holmes conceded, lowering his voice after the man had again withdrawn. "In point of fact, the buildings in question have been extensively renovated, as I have taken pains to ascertain. Because of the, um, event that transpired at Number 3, folk have been perhaps understandably reluctant to put up there and, as a consequence, the new owner has been obliged to perform substantial alterations. The entire block has been renovated with new flooring, plaster, fresh paint inside and out, more tasteful wallpaper, and wonderfully attractive curtains."

"All of which changes nothing," I insisted sourly.

"Perhaps not the wallpaper," the detective allowed, "but the block is decidedly more attractive than it was, with the addition of new, built-in closets, including one in the bedroom at Number 3, ideal for our purposes. You, doctor," he added, pointing to me with his fork, "will lie concealed within, close at hand to overhear and, if necessary, intervene."

"And just what is it *I* am to do?" asked Juliet. She was torn, I could see, between apprehension and the thrill of the chase, sensations with which I was more than familiar.

Holmes proffered a smile that struck me as unmistakably false. "All Miss Packwood must do is sit quietly in the nearby dining room."

It occurred to me the detective had indeed run out of ideas to find himself reduced to this expedient.

"That sounds simple enough," Juliet said, but a note of unease crept into her voice and served to replenish my misgivings.

"And how am I supposed to know when, like a jack-in-the-box, I am to pop from my place of concealment?"

He favored me with solemn look. "You will know, Watson." The aroma of fresh coffee had the curious effect of rendering his assurances more plausible.

"And what of you?" I softened my tone, which, I realized, had become shrill. "What is to be your role in this jerry-rigged enterprise?"

"I have made all the necessary arrangements," he answered serenely.

I can scarcely bear to revisit the imperceptible degrees by which I was compelled to give ground. Juliet was by now in thrall to Sherlock Holmes, not after any romantic inclination (as her reassuring smiles directed to me made clear) but plainly (and naively) she regarded the detective's proposal as the sort of adventure women were routinely denied. By now I knew the high-spirited girl well enough to comprehend she was likely picturing herself as another Nellie Bly.[*] The fact that we were attempting to snare an actual murderer was not yet real to her.

Sensing victory, Holmes played his part smoothly, suddenly effusive over my case histories, predicting what a feather in my cap this account would make. I would like to claim this clumsy stratagem carried no weight but am ashamed to own that perhaps it did. At all events, after another hour waging a fruitless rear-guard action, I capitulated.

---

[*] Nellie Bly was the pen name of intrepid American journalist, Nellie Cochrane Seaman, who made headlines by having herself certified insane so as to expose the inhumane treatment of inmates at the asylum on Blackwell's Island in New York. Later, she beat the record set by Jules Verne's hero, Phileas Fogg, circling the world in less than eighty days.

"You give your solemn assurance no one will be harmed?"

Holmes struggled to suppress a sigh of relief. "I have taken every precaution," he repeated. "What do you say, my dear fellow? The game's afoot."

I looked at Juliet. Like the detective, she was plainly eager to hear my views. I did not like to disappoint either of them. "Very well."

"You agree to the plan?" Holmes attempted unsuccessfully to keep his excitement in check.

"That is what I seem to have said," I replied, avoiding Juliet's eyes.

Not even Sherlock Holmes could have foreseen the consequences of that fateful decision.

It took another week to complete our arrangements. An estate agent concluded an agreement for one Violet Hamilton to sign a six-month lease for Number 3, Lauriston Gardens. The surprisingly scrupulous agent took it upon himself to notify the young woman of the place's unsavory history and duly cautioned her, but Violet Hamilton (the name supplied by the detective), not to be dissuaded, was deaf to his warnings and my misgivings. Juliet Packwood signed her alias on the agreement he put before her.

On those interim occasions when we were alone together, as if by mutual consent, we avoided discussion of the course we had decided upon, almost as if we declined to allude to the weather amid a typhoon.

And so it was that on the first of April, my service revolver bulging in the pocket of my Norfolk, I found myself crammed within the newly installed closet in the bedroom of Number 3, Lauriston Gardens.

In the adjacent sitting room, Juliet sat primly near her large, unwieldy trunk.

April Fools' Day indeed. The stage was set. The actors and props were in their places. All was in readiness for the curtain to rise. It wanted only the entrance of the leading player.

The interior of the closet was stifling. I wished I had shed my jacket before entombing myself, but I had not taken into account how much time must pass in those close quarters before I could escape to open air.

Juliet, in the next room, was too distant for me to detect the sound of her breathing; the best I could hope for in the stillness was to make out the faint rustle of her dress as she occasionally shifted her position. Once I thought I heard her cough.

How long must our tableaux be maintained? In the darkness, it was impossible to gauge the passage of time. Only the increasing ache in my leg hinted at the length of my stay. The sounds of distant traffic on the Brixton Road grew and diminished as the rush hour waxed and waned, finally subsiding into a queasy silence, broken only by the occasional rumble of a delivery wagon and the heavy clomping of draft horse hooves. I was not unaccustomed to such vigils and could remember with little difficulty the watch Holmes and I kept in the bowels of the City and Suburban Bank, as we awaited the appearance of the infamous John Clay as he tunneled into the vault from below, hoping to lay hands on the bank's millions.*

But in the stygian gloom my thoughts now stretched back still further, to the only previous occasion when I had set foot in these

---

* As recounted in "The Adventure of the Red-Headed League."

once-dilapidated rooms, the very first time I accompanied my singular friend on one of his baffling inquiries. It seemed only yesterday, amid peeling strips of garish wallpaper, when I found myself staring at the snarling face of the corpse on Number 3's dining room floor, mere minutes before Holmes discovered the word *Rache* written in blood on a nearby wall. It was then and there he first demonstrated to me his unique gifts. In the dark of the closet, I realized I was smiling at the recollection. The police were convinced the murderer had begun to write the name Rachel but fled before he'd finished. They were certain a woman by that name would ultimately figure in the case before Holmes, greatly amused, pointed out that *Rache* was German for revenge. I mused on the detective's notion that art requires a frame. Was Holmes including the art of detection as well?

More time passed. My leg was throbbing in earnest now. Attempting to hold myself in readiness, I sought to recall all I had I seen before closing the closet door and enveloping myself in darkness. True, the rooms at Number 3 were presently redecorated, though the work had been done on the cheap. My hiding place, as an example, was a flimsy construction of pine slats that squeaked at my slightest movement. The empty hangers that floated on the clothing bar clacked whenever they chanced to come into contact with my head. My strength taxed to the utmost, at length I was compelled to ease my weight from one foot to the other. The closet creaked like a ship at sea, causing me to freeze. How far had the sound traveled? In the next room, had Juliet heard and was she now worried on my account in addition to her own? There was no way of knowing.

Is it possible that I managed to fall asleep on my feet? Only the *clop-clop* of an approaching carriage served to jolt me to sudden wakefulness. As I strained to hear, the hoofbeats stopped. Was it my fancy that I could make out the faint jingle of a harness as the horse shook its head, followed by the slam of a carriage door?

I was once more desperate to shift the weight to my stronger leg, but dared not move. I now heard the creak of the entry door. This was followed by some sounds I was unable to identify, followed in turn by a voice I knew at once.

"Miss Hamilton?"

"Lady Glendenning. I am sorry to have inconvenienced you." Juliet's voice was louder than normal for my benefit.

"What seems to be the trouble?" the voice of our erstwhile client was asking. "Something amiss with the premises?"

"No, nothing amiss. That is . . ."

"Yes?"

"I am sorry," this from Juliet. "I'm afraid. It's just that—well, I've changed my mind."

"Oh?" Was it my imagination or did the speaker's soft monosyllable convey ominous displeasure?

"I know. I'm frightfully embarrassed but—"

"Has to it do with what happened—?"

"Happened here? Years ago? Goodness no. I was told about it, of course, but it's nothing like that, your ladyship. Nothing at all. It's just that, well, it's too far from the Underground."

"The Underground?"

"I've only just realized." Juliet was speaking more quickly now. "At night I shouldn't like to make the walk. I hope you understand."

Except for her breathless intonation, the brave girl was playing her role to perfection. There was silence, followed by slow footsteps. I could picture Lady Glendenning pacing as she gathered her thoughts.

"You did sign a lease, Miss Hamilton," she spoke so softly I could barely make out the words.

"I know, I'm dreadfully sorry, but it just won't do."

There was another silence. No footfalls now. Then a sigh. "Very well, we shall tear up the lease and consider the matter closed. And now, as it's late—"

"There's just one more difficulty, your ladyship, I'm so sorry to bring it up—"

"And what is that, Miss Hamilton?" Now the sound of impatience was easy to detect.

"My portmanteau."

"Your—"

"My trunk."

"This trunk?"

"Yes. The cabman brought it in and now of course he's gone. I'm so sorry—"

"I'm afraid I don't quite—"

"If you could ask your driver to help bring it back to the Brixton Road, I'm sure I can flag a cab for myself."

Another silence before—

"My driver."

"If you wouldn't mind. I am so very—"

"Miss Hamilton, this is very tiresome. I've had a long day and—"

"I know." Juliet's voice was the essence of contrition. "I've made such a mess of things. I do apologize."

Another silence. Followed by an exasperated sigh.

"Very well. Wait here."

The door was slammed harder than necessary, a sign of her irritation, as the woman went to fetch her coachman.

Another silence. Inside the closet I was drenched in sweat as my fingers crept toward the pocket of my coat. Where was Sherlock Holmes? Why in heaven's name had I ever agreed to participate in the detective's plan? It was cold comfort to remind myself I had had no say in the matter. The choice had been Juliet's and she had been adamant in her determination to participate.

Now approaching footsteps were audible, a man's hobnail boots slapping on the cobblestones. The door opened and almost at once I heard cries of mutual surprise.

"Miss Packwood!" from the man.

"Miss *Packwood*—?" from Lady Glendenning.

"Dear God!" from Juliet.

Holmes was correct. I knew my cue when I heard it and burst from my closet even as Sherlock Holmes sprang from the unlocked trunk.

"I take it you are the late Rupert Milestone," he said, addressing the astonished coachman.

Lady Glendenning instantly made for the door, only to find it blocked by Inspector Gregson attired in mufti, even as several police and Inspector Lestrade appeared at the window. Holmes had indeed made his arrangements.

"I didn't kill him!' cried the artist, eyes bulging as he looked wildly about.

Lady Glendenning, strands of her white-gold hair tumbling in disarray, clapped both hands over her face as though to render herself invisible.

"Lord Southbank? No, you did not kill him. But you did attempt to trample me with your cab as I left Signor Garibaldi's residence on Cheyne Walk," Holmes reminded him. "And you did return later with Lady Glendenning where she used her passkey to unlock the conservatory door at the rear of Number 12 and turn on the gas, smothering Signor Garibaldi and his housekeeper." He turned to the cowering woman. "Lady Glendenning, you are a far more accomplished actress than you gave yourself credit for."

The woman said nothing, but glared with blazing eyes at Holmes from behind her spread fingers, one of which still displayed the outsized garnet ring.

"What have you done with the razor you fetched to cut Lord Southbank's throat, as he struggled with Mr. Milestone in his studio the night of the blizzard?" the detective continued. "We have been unable to find it."

The only sound in the electric silence that followed was Vera Pertwee Glendenning's struggle for breath as she lowered her hands, and with jerky, silent movements, probed her reticule.

"I have it here," she said quietly, producing the missing item and looking at the detective. Her complexion, drained of colour, was a waxy white, almost matching the razor's ivory handle. "You must understand," she said with surprising calm, "Lord Southbank had the upper hand." A glistening film of perspiration shone on her forehead, eerily reminding me of varnish. "He was going to kill

Freddie. I had to do *something*. Can you help me, Mr. Holmes? I came to you for help," she reminded him.

Holmes forced himself to look at Juliet, whom Lady Glendenning had well and truly avenged. He swallowed with difficulty.

"Lady Glendenning, I cannot help you," he said.

She closed her eyes and nodded, having anticipated his answer. In another moment I half expected to see the beaded moisture on her forehead congeal like craquelure.

"Then I must help myself."

Even as Rupert Milestone screamed, "No!" and flung himself forward, hurling shrieking Juliet headfirst into the wall, Vera Pertwee used the blade as she had used it once before.

13

UNTANGLING THE SKEIN

"**I** can never forgive myself," said Sherlock Holmes.

"You gave your word no one would be harmed," I seethed.

"I know, Watson. Great heavens, I know."

We looked up as footsteps were heard walking down the hospital corridor.

"I've given Miss Packwood laudanum," the doctor informed us. "I believe her uncle has been notified and is on his way,"

"Will she—?"

"She has a bruise on her forehead from her collision with the wall and will likely feel groggy with an aching head when she wakes, but that won't be until morning. I see no indication of a concussion but believe we should keep her under observation overnight. Otherwise, she appears unharmed and in no imminent danger."

"But she was," I insisted mulishly to myself. Aloud I merely said, "I will be here," gazing dully at the frosted window opposite the bench on which we sat. From the corner of my eye, I saw the doctor glance at the detective.

Holmes was staring at the linoleum floor.

"Very well." After a further hesitation, the physician's footsteps retreated the way they had come.

I said nothing, too exhausted by the appalling events of the past—how long had it been, mere hours?—when Holmes had carried Juliet from the sight of the dying woman as I futilely attempted to save her life. It was the second time the cursed room had been stained with blood—only this time it was more than mere writing on the wall.

Holmes remained beside me on the hard wood bench as the hours crawled by. We could neither of us think of anything to say.

By nightfall, Gerald Packwood arrived from Swiss Cottage. I roused myself and in disjointed sentences managed to give him an account of the debacle.

"Did the doctor offer a prognosis?" was all the poor man managed to ask.

"Not in so many words. We are ascertaining whether there has been a concussion."

"I wish to see her."

"Of course." Leaving the immobile Holmes, I led Juliet's uncle to her room. One of the sisters sat keeping watch on the patient, whose features were briefly illumined by the hall lights when we entered. I drew a sharp breath at the sight of my poor, pale love.

"Close the door, please," the nurse whispered. "The corridor is noisy."

I obeyed. In the darkened room, aside from nighttime traffic below the window, the only sound was Juliet's shallow breathing.

"Any change, sister?"

"No change," she murmured.

For the better part of a minute we stared in silence at the sleeping beauty.

"My niece is a strong and capable young woman," Packwood seemingly addressed himself.

"That she is," I agreed reverently.

I could not tell if he heard me. Left unspoken was the question of whether Juliet's strength would see her through to anything like a full recovery.

Seeing there was nothing to be done at this juncture, I gently tugged the art dealer by the sleeve. He allowed me to pull him from the room, shutting the door quietly behind us. Momentarily at a loss as to what to do or where to go, he stood irresolutely in the corridor before finally focusing his attention on me. At length I succeeded in looking him in the eye.

"She has spoken of you," he said, finally.

Taking in his frank and open features, I was able, with some effort, to picture the resemblance to the elder brother with whom I had served in Afghanistan.

"Favorably, I hope."

Before he could reply, Holmes, unshaven, with red-rimmed eyes, joined us. "How is she?"

"Mr. Packwood, may I introduce you to Sherlock Holmes? It was he who carried your niece from the room at the time of the, uh—"

"You have my gratitude, sir." Mercifully, he did not allude to the circumstances that had placed his niece in the room in question.

The detective shrank into himself like a scalded cat. "I cannot forgive myself," he repeated.

Packwood turned to me.

"I will stay with her," I assured him. "She is in good hands here at the Royal Marsden and I am myself a doctor. There is nothing more to be done tonight."

He considered this. "You will keep me apprised of developments?" Then, struck by another thought, he added, "Someone must see to Oedipus. I expect the landlady will admit me."

"Oedipus?"

"Eddy-Puss," he stressed the syllables. "Her cat."

I had to smile at Juliet's whimsy. "I will not leave her side. You have my word."

He eyed me, still governed by conflicting impulses. "Very well. I will return in the morning."

Once more words failed us. After another pause, Packwood walked quietly away. The sight of his stiff, retreating form caused me to close my eyes.

My profession and status at the hospital entitled me to certain privileges and I did not hesitate to exploit them. I assumed the nurse's place by Juliet's bed. She woke uncertainly the following morning, but her eyes were able to follow the movements of my finger, an encouraging sign. She swallowed some tea and nibbled a bit of muffin, before falling asleep once more. I remained seated and kept hold of her hand. I did not know where Holmes was nor what he was doing and, to be candid, I didn't think to inquire.

The following day I was permitted to take Juliet back to Goodge Street. She stared silently out the carriage window, as if seeing the world for the first time. At a loss for words, I did not like to break in upon her thoughts but contented myself with taking her inert hand.

In Goodge Street, under the landlady's watchful eye, I lay Juliet down and drew up the coverlet. Instantly a large Abyssinian sprang onto the pillow beside her head, purring contentedly as it settled in its accustomed place.

"Eddy-Puss." Juliet's hand groped for the animal's shoulders and rested there. Her touch seemed to reassure them both and the landlady withdrew.

"I have sent word to your uncle, who will be here shortly," I whispered to Juliet, adjusting the pillow and stroking her forehead. The cat glared at my ministrations from his perch, briefly hissed, and made a show of teeth.

"It's all right, James," she rasped, her eyes still shut. "The fault is none of yours." Her left hand once more reached for mine. Her grasp was weak but she offered a faint smile. "As a free agent, I made my own decision and must deal with the consequences. Which is as it should be." She yawned.

"Dearest, try to—"

"And it must be said," she added, yawning once more, "Sherlock Holmes's plan was successful. Sir Johnny's killer was apprehended."

"Two killers," I quietly corrected her. "Holmes is distraught."

"No one compelled me to participate," Juliet reiterated, closing her eyes. What I took to be a cough was in fact a shaky laugh. "What did I think was going to happen? That they would meekly surrender and confess?"

I drew my chair closer. "Try to rest, dearest."

She pressed my hand. "I want to know what happened, James."

"When you're stronger, my love."

Juliet's recovery from the sensational events in which she had played a crucial role was neither easy nor short. Her chief symptom, once the drug's effects had dissipated, was an inability to sleep; when she did, the tragedy at Lauriston Gardens invariably replayed itself, or if it did not, her terror of such a repetition prevented her getting any rest. I did not judge it prudent to dose her with more laudanum. By night the lights were always on and at such times the woman clung to my hand with a febrile intensity. The cat, as if sensing her distress, seldom left her side. When at last she slept, I dared not move for fear she would wake and find me gone. I returned to Baker Street only when, in a fitful slumber, she released her grasp.

At Baker Street, I had another patient. I found myself assuming something of Doktor Freud's role as I understood it,* listening to the worries and meditations of not one but two convalescents. There was little I could do but I have always been an attentive listener and, as I discovered, listening in itself can prove therapeutic.

---

*   A full account of Holmes and Watson's time with Sigmund Freud in Vienna may be found in *The Seven-Per-Cent Solution*. Not published until after Freud's death in 1939, it was, in Holmes's judgment, a tale for which the world was not yet prepared.

Holmes had the harder task, for it was pointless to deny his role in the catastrophe. Again and again, I was obliged to remain silent as he obsessively replayed his part in the business, interrupting only on occasion to remind him that Juliet, not he, had made the choice to participate.

"An uninformed choice," he mumbled, slumping in his chair.

But as her uncle maintained—and I by now was able to confirm—Juliet Packwood was composed of stronger stuff than her delicate features suggested. After a slow start, she looked to be on the way to a complete recovery. As spring arrived in earnest, sleep came more easily. I coaxed her for walks and we basked in warm sunshine. It was mid-May when, on another visit to the zoo, she found herself laughing at the antics of two frolicking apes. She looked at me and I understood then it was time for her questions to be answered.

"We have two interlocking narratives," began Sherlock Holmes as we four convened the following Monday in Baker Street. Juliet and her uncle had joined us for tea and explanations. Holmes was thinner and paler than usual, but only an occasional hesitation betrayed the effects of recent events. Juliet, by contrast, appeared fully in control of her faculties. Her uncle's estimation of his niece's resilient constitution was proving correct.

"Two narratives?" Gerald Packwood asked, setting down his cup.

Holmes nodded. "The first involves young Vera Pertwee, a typist and sometime actress, who married Basil Lord Glendenning, a wealthy widower and property owner, following a fortuitous meeting, the result of a downpour in Putney. For all we know, the marriage was happy, or at all events, uneventful. I know of nothing to suggest otherwise, though the absence of progeny may be a point worth noting."

"But obviously—" I interjected.

"Ah, yes, Watson, 'obviously.' Obviously something intervened to alter the status quo."

"And that was—?"

"Basil Glendenning's decision to have a portrait painted of his attractive young wife. In one of his periodic fits of parsimony, he chose the poor man's Sargent for the job, which is how Lady Glendenning and Rupert Milestone chanced to meet. What followed is perhaps best explained in terms of chemistry."

"I beg your pardon?" Packwood cast a sideways look at his niece.

"Chemistry," repeated the detective. "Imagine two substances, each, on its own, inert, but combine them and the result is combustible. There is a French name for what followed but let me save that tidbit for later. Rupert Milestone, whose true name turns out to have been the rather unpropitious Fred Millstone, had altered the spelling of his surname and re-anointed himself Rupert, doubtless to add a bit of swagger. He and Lady Glendenning (née Vera Pertwee of Islington) found they had much in common. Both were attractive and ambitious, both intent on surmounting humble origins. Somewhere (if they didn't destroy it to conceal all evidence of the connection that joined them), we shall beyond question unearth the original portrait that brought about their fateful encounter." He turned to me. "Watson, you may recall my observation that with his extraordinary looks, many of Milestone's sitters were likely to be women."

"Yes, I remember." Where Juliet Packwood was concerned, I was myself familiar with chemistry.

"Do you also remember the large, pale square of wall in Lady Glendenning's office when she presented me with a cheque for our rather marginal services?" Holmes asked me.

"I do, now you mention it, though I confess I did not register it at the time."

"One must not only observe, one must *see*," the detective admonished. "I have little doubt the original Milestone portrait of Vera Pertwee once graced that blank space of wall."

"And then what?" Juliet spoke for the first time.

Holmes paused to light his pipe, giving Juliet and, in particular, her bewildered uncle, time to absorb his narrative before resuming it. "With the painting of her portrait commenced an intrigue. Milestone, with his splendid wardrobe and virile appearance, was difficult to resist. And when Basil Lord Glendenning obligingly succumbed to age or illness, his merry widow, if I may appropriate the term, expressed her grief by dyeing her hair blonde."

"As in the play?"

"Precisely, Watson. 'Her hair has turned quite gold with grief.' Oscar Wilde knew whereof he spoke. Unlike Her Majesty, perpetually mourning the Prince Consort, I wager there's more than one widow who has responded to the passing of a less than satisfactory spouse with some harmless capers, such as lightening the colour of her hair. It was your offhand recollection of the clever line in the play that served to unlock the puzzle and caused me to chew apart my pipe stem."

I turned to Juliet with a smile. "It seems I am 'not luminous, but a conductor of light.'"

"A very able conductor," she agreed, taking my hand in hers once more before turning back to the detective. "But isn't it possible the affair between Milestone and Lady Glendenning did not begin until after her husband's death?"

"That is doubtless a more pleasing notion," Holmes conceded, "but I think we may conclude from the dark hairs on the brush found in the artist's locked linen chest that they had become intimate long before the lady decided to lighten the colour of her hair."

"Oh, I see." I could sense Juliet's disappointment. She wanted, at the least, to believe Vera Pertwee had been a faithful wife.

Holmes hesitated. He had no wish to provoke any sort of relapse.

Juliet perceived his reluctance and offered a rueful smile. "You needn't be afraid, Mr. Holmes. Better for me to know than guess."

The detective looked to Gerald Packwood. Satisfied the art dealer, desirous of learning what had happened, was not about to call a halt to his recital, he took a breath. I knew Holmes well enough to understand he longed to summarize the chain of reasoning that led to his conclusions. And perhaps expiate some of his guilt into the bargain.

"Very well," he resumed. "In headlong commemoration or celebration of their intimacy, Lady Glendenning's lover now painted a second portrait for their private enjoyment, this one inspired by Manet's scandalous nude. Among other secret salutations, he preserved his mistress's blue eyes instead of Manet's dark ones and he couldn't resist reproducing the attractive mole on Vera Pertwee's cheek."

"Neither of which is to be found in Manet's original *Olympia*." It was clear Juliet enjoyed piecing together the links in the chain.

"Correct, Miss Packwood. In addition, Milestone originally included the lady's newly blonde tresses, but about which he or his mistress subsequently had second thoughts."

"Pentimento," Juliet happily recalled.

"Precisely."

"I'm not sure I follow," said Gerald Packwood.

"That is understandable," the detective assured him, shaking out a second match. "But while the second painting, with its frankly erotic subject matter, was intended as an intimate message for the lovers only, Milestone, or possibly Vera, worried that a chance discovery of the picture would expose their liaison."

I suddenly understood. "And so the painter darkened her newly blonde hair and for good measure excised her beauty mark as well, but he left her blue eyes as he knew and loved them."

"Correct," Holmes nodded approvingly.

I stole a look at Juliet, gratified to see my reasoning had impressed her.

"Excellent, Watson. And, as a final precaution, the picture was consigned to a locked linen chest in Milestone's bedroom, only to be displayed on occasion for the lovers' delectation."

Gerald Packwood frowned. "But what has all this to do with Lord Southbank?"

"Ah," returned Holmes, "that is where the second narrative intersects the first. In the initial, frenzied flush of their affair, Rupert Milestone neglected to inform his paramour he was being blackmailed."

"Blackmailed?" This was not what the art dealer expected to hear.

"Blackmailed by his employer, Sir Johnny Van Dam," Juliet explained, shuddering at memories of her own.

"Why and what with?" Packwood was perplexed.

"Sir Johnny, overextended and desperate for inventory, was squeezing his restorer for more and more old masters to market," Holmes explained. "If Milestone refused to oblige, Van Dam threatened to denounce his employee as a gifted forger, protest he'd been deceived, and so forth." He glanced at Juliet. "A dangerous man to cross, as I think we have stipulated."

Juliet looked at her feet and said nothing.

Satisfied, the detective resumed. "The painter was trapped. Recall, for Milestone it wasn't simply a matter of painting faster; he had to locate and acquire sixteenth or seventeenth century pictures poor enough in quality or condition he could afford. After obtaining such a canvas, he had to pumice off the painting to obtain an authentic blank on which to apply fresh gesso, or else, if pressed for time, to forgo entirely that laborious chore and paint directly on top of the old picture, always a risk, should the original somehow peep through. Doubtless the slower, more cumbersome method was safer. After the gesso, Milestone could then paint *à la manière de*, using his phenol and formaldehyde concoction, which allowed for no mistakes, to ensure convincing hardness. But if Sir Johnny's goose didn't lay golden eggs more speedily, he might well go to prison, forced to assume the fall for his desperate but well-regarded employer. On the other hand, if he obliged and worked too swiftly, he ran the risk of his handiwork being labeled pyrite."

"Pyrite?"

"Fool's gold, Miss Packwood. Fake. From Milestone's perspective it wasn't much of a choice. He succumbed to extortion so as to afford his wardrobe and his mistress." Holmes sat back as a new thought occurred to him. "One hesitates to contemplate the number of exquisite forgeries that are currently greeted with gasps of admiration in great houses and museums around the world, all the handiwork of overworked Freddie Millstone."

I could see from Juliet's look the idea and extent of Milestone's deception was a sobering one.

"But eventually Milestone had to tell Vera what was going on," I hazarded.

"Correct. Either he found himself obliged to tell or Lady Glendenning learned of his situation by chance, but it amounted to the same thing."

Holmes's summary sparked a memory and I turned to Juliet. "Didn't you once tell me something about Sir Johnny not being so foolhardy as to sully his hands with paint?"

She smiled. "So I did. I compared his hands with those of Pontius Pilate. Something of an exaggeration, perhaps, but not entirely wide of the mark. Artists and preservationists may have paint under their nails—but Lord Southbank would make sure his hands were always lily white."

Her own complexion reddened as she said this. Lord Southbank's hands had not remained white.

Holmes took a breath and effected a diversion from this troublesome territory. "It was the fact that the snowman's corpse had no trace of paint that first struck me as irregular." He paused once more. "Which brings us to the night in question and a *folie à deux*."

"What night in question?" demanded Gerald Packwood, even as I asked, "What do you mean by folly—what was it?"

"*À deux*, Mr. Packwood. The French expression I promised when we sat down, coined not so long ago by the psychologist and neurologist, Ernest-Charles Lasègue. *Folie à deux* roughly translates as 'a madness shared by two.'"

"I've never heard of such a thing."

The detective smiled. "I doubt you would have come across it in your world, Mr. Packwood. Alienists have characterized it as a delusional belief somehow transmitted from one individual to another. In this instance, decisions were made by Vera Pertwee, whose dominant personality held sway over the more malleable Freddie Millstone. Under her influence, both became convinced they were invulnerable."

"It seems strange for Milestone to fall so under her spell," Juliet mused, "he looked so—"

"Attractive, Miss Packwood?" Holmes supplied, glancing at me. "Unlike painting, it is never a good idea to judge a book by its cover. Looks do not equal intelligence, nor does intelligence translate to either courage or virtue. I've known complete dolts whose features give every appearance of high intellect."

"You're saying the woman practiced her wiles on him?" I was struggling to follow Holmes's explanation.

"Vera Pertwee had plenty of practice and no shortage of wiles," he answered dryly. "Remember, she was an actress. The damsel in distress ruse has pulled the wool over the eyes of many otherwise clear-sighted men, present company not excepted," he scowled, crooking a forefinger toward himself.

"Please answer my question," Packwood persisted. "What night in question are we talking about and what happened on that night?"

Holmes stole another look at Juliet who calmly withstood his scrutiny. "Very well. Once Milestone confided his difficulties to Vera, she assumed the lead in resolving them. She urged her lover to invite Lord Southbank to his studio with a view to settling their differences. It was her conviction that following a rational discussion, a new agreement could be reached that would satisfy both parties. The tractable Milestone and the desperate Sir Johnny agreed to this and a meeting was duly arranged."

I was tempted to raise my hand like a schoolboy. "But things did not go as planned and matters fell out as you described when we first visited the studio, Holmes."

"Correct again, doctor. Lady Glendenning underestimated the passions on both sides—on the one hand, Milestone's fury at the miserly treatment and humiliating pressure he was under from Sir Johnny to produce short-order masterpieces, and, on the other, Lord Southbank's dire financial straits and history of brawling from his early days peddling tinware on the streets of Brussels. Words between the two high-strung, hot-tempered men soon led to blows."

"Between Rupert Milestone and Sir Jonathan Van Dam?" Gerald Packwood was incredulous.

"Yes, and Sir Johnny, physically larger of the two, clearly had the upper hand in their fisticuffs, at which point panicked Lady Glendenning fled to the bathroom and returned with the razor and—" he broke off as Juliet gasped. "Miss Packwood—"

"Holmes, I think we'd best save the rest for another—"

"I'm quite all right," Juliet insisted, briefly compressing her lips. "Pray continue, Mr. Holmes."

"Are you sure?" the detective glanced at me.

"Quite sure," Juliet answered before I could reply. Her pressure on my hand was now intense but plainly signaled the young woman's determination to hear everything.

Holmes took a breath and continued his summary. "It was after Lady Glendenning's—let us for the moment call it, 'action'—it was after Lady Glendenning's action that she once more made the decisions and the suggestible Milestone again followed her lead. As we have seen, originality was not his strong suit. He was ever the copycat."

"What decisions do you refer to?" I asked.

"How to conceal the crime, Watson. Her mind doubtless racing, Lady Glendenning nonetheless felt she had a strong hand to play: she was a gifted actress in possession of a substantial fortune and an enormous collection of latchkeys. Having noted the leonine, tawny-haired resemblance between the two men"—here he turned to Juliet once more—"I believe when you were posing for Milestone's Botticelli and overheard them argue, you compared both to a pair of strutting roosters, Miss Packwood?—Lady Glendenning conceived her daring solution to the night's unforeseen outcome. Milestone would change identities with the dead man. Or rather, the dead man would assume Milestone's identity. The victim's clothes were removed and he was dragged to the wash basin where his beard was shaved, increasing their similarity—"

"And leaving longer than usual shaving hairs in the basin," I noted.

"Just so. After which, Van Dam's body was re-clothed in apparel from the artist's Savile Row wardrobe. What you mistook for postmortem bloating, explaining the tight fit, Watson, was in reality the difference between the dimensions of the combatants. Lord Southbank, as we've noted, was slightly larger than Rupert Milestone."

"Especially his feet!" I now understood the reason behind the missing footwear.

"Correct, yet again, doctor. Van Dam's feet were too large to fit in any of Milestone's shoes and so when he was immured as a snowman that night during the blizzard (at which time the streets were conveniently deserted), his black-stockinged feet remained unshod. But you were mistaken in your assumption that bending forward after he was attacked preserved Rupert Milestone's Prince Albert Frock coat from bloodstains. The coat and waistcoat had not yet been fetched from Milestone's wardrobe and placed on Lord Southbank's body, and for this reason they escaped any—"

"I wonder if you have something stronger than tea," Juliet asked, her voice pitched higher than usual.

"My dear—" began her uncle.

Holmes sprang to his feet. "Let me fetch you some brandy," he offered.

"Juliet—" again began Packwood, but she held up her other hand. "I assure you, uncle, I'm perfectly well. I could just do with some fortification."

Holmes returned with the brandy. She took the snifter and held the amber liquid up for inspection. "I don't believe I've ever tasted brandy," she confessed.

"You'll find a little goes a long way," I told her. There was silence as she took a sip, then coughed, handing the drink to her uncle.

"How right you are, dearest."

"Juliet—"

"Do continue, Mr. Holmes, but please answer one question first."

"If I can, Miss Packwood."

"Why did Lady Glendenning go to the police in the first place? Surely it made no sense to call to their attention the events at Number 7, Turncoat Lane."

"An excellent question. In point of fact, I very much doubt such a course of action occurred to her in the immediate aftermath of the, ahem, event." The detective, satisfied an outburst was not forthcoming, proceeded to knock the ashes from his pipe. "At first the lovers believed themselves secure. The winter was harsh, still more snow was in the offing. It would be some time before Lord Southbank's body was discovered and then it would be mistaken for that of the painter."

"And in the meantime," I interposed, "Van Dam's employees, ignorant and anxious as to his whereabouts, were understandably keen not to acknowledge anything amiss. You will recall gatekeeper Foggerty's declaration, 'You've just missed him,' his spur of the moment inspiration to conceal the fact that no one at Van Dam's knew where Sir Johnny had got to. Better to claim he was merely 'out of town.'"

"But then—" prompted Gerald Packwood, draining the remaining contents in the snifter.

"But then," the detective resumed, "as time passed and she gave more thought to the matter, Lady Glendenning realized her difficulties were not at an end. She *had* to go the police."

"I don't follow," said the art dealer, setting down the empty glass.

"She had no choice! She had to play her part. A landlord whose tenant was behind on his rent as months went by? It would appear irregular at best not to report her concerns to the authorities. It was exceptionally cunning on Lady Glendenning's part to realize this. At the very least she was on record as having reported the disappearance of her tenant, and if the worst came to the worst when the body was discovered, her acting abilities would serve her well were she asked to confirm the dead man's identity, as indeed she was. What actress could resist such a scene? The shock! The collapse! After that final performance, Vera Pertwee Glendenning was doubtless entitled to assume her role in the business would be at an end."

"What went wrong?" Juliet asked.

"Sherlock Holmes did," I answered.

The detective inclined his head in my direction. "I believe Dr. Watson sums it up. When she called on them, the police were inclined to dismiss Lady Glendenning's concerns, as she hoped they would, but a helpful Inspector Gregson attempted to mollify her worries by suggesting she consult a detective, understandably recommending myself. Lady Glendenning now found herself obliged to knock at my door and matters unfolded from there."

There was a silence as we digested this information. I now recalled how uncomfortable Lady Glendenning had appeared when she first visited our rooms. At the time I had ascribed this to the nervousness many clients feel when first consulting a detective; it is likely an awkward experience, one in which potentially embarrassing matters must inevitably come to light. But now I knew better. Viewed in retrospect, Lady Glendenning's was the demeanor of someone trapped. The last thing she wished was to find herself forced to employ Sherlock Holmes, but appearances demanded she do as the helpful Inspector Gregson had suggested.

"'*Oh, what tangled webs we weave, when first we practice to deceive.*' I had come across that couplet somewhere and now found myself speaking the lines aloud.*

"Ah yes, Watson. Lady Glendenning found herself on a train moving so speedily she had no way of disembarking. She tried to slow the train with her fanciful tale of Milestone having a brother somewhere in Shropshire, but that wild goose chase led the police nowhere very quickly and the train she was on resumed its fateful speed."

More silence followed. Juliet appeared to study her fingernails. "It appears I owe Lady Glendenning a great deal," she said in a low voice.

Evidently she had never spoken to her uncle of what had taken place between her and Lord Southbank when the two were alone, for he went on, clearly ignorant of the oblique reference.

"And what of Milestone?" the art dealer demanded. "Has he confirmed any of this to the police?"

"He has not and likely cannot. Since his arrest on the night in question, according to Inspector Lestrade, the wretched man has become entirely catatonic."

"I beg your pardon?"

"Catatonia, a condition, sometimes permanent, wherein the sufferer is unable to speak or respond. Remember my description of *folie à deux*, a shared madness. Milestone was by this point wholly

---

* Walter Scott's *Marmion*.

dependent on Vera. Without her, he has become a marionette whose strings have been severed."

"Could he be shamming?" I wondered.

"If he is, time will reveal it," the detective returned. "The man will be under constant observation. The least deviation in his symptoms will instantly change his fate."

This was followed by another silence.

"Why didn't they simply go abroad?" Juliet mused.

"Another good question," the detective allowed. "Money was certainly part of the difficulty. Milestone's bank account was off-limits, for a start. Any attempt to extract funds from that source would instantly set off alarm bells."

"But he had secreted funds at his studio," I remembered.

"True. And so he staged what was meant to look like a robbery. He retrieved the banknotes you and I had so virtuously replaced, Watson. That's what first suggested to me the painter was alive. Only the man who'd hidden the money would know where to look for it. And where *not* to look for it."

"How do you mean?" Packwood demanded. I could see him struggling to assimilate a flood of information that was swamping him.

"There was a padlocked linen chest on the premises which the thief did not bother to crack, for the simple reason he knew there was no cash within it."

"But Lady Glendenning was very well provided for," I objected. "She could have given him plenty of money and never missed it."

Holmes smiled. "Yes, but with money she would have surrendered control. In a *folie à deux*, both parties are mutually dependent.

Just as Milestone was in her thrall, Lady Glendenning was by now equally reliant on the painter and not about to enfranchise her mirrored self by providing him any means that might lead to his independence. In their disordered thinking, they might as well have been joined by handcuffs."

"But how could such an arrangement endure?" I asked. "The man could hardly have set foot inside her house without occasioning remark."

"There the lady displayed her fullest ingenuity," the detective returned with grudging admiration. "Driving a team was a skill known to Milestone from his bucolic childhood. By making him her coachman, he could live in the adjacent mews, unnoticed by anyone in society who might recognize him. By night she could visit as she pleased. The furtive necessity of clandestine meetings in the stables may have added a certain piquancy to their rendezvous, while by day, swathed in his yellow muffler, he could anonymously drive her everywhere."

"Such as the time he attempted to run you over," I supplied.

"*What?*" niece and uncle exclaimed simultaneously.

"I fear I very much deserved such a fate," Holmes conceded with a heavy sigh. "After I revealed my identity to Signor Garibaldi."

"I'm sorry to appear dense," Packwood protested, "but at this point I've not the least idea what you're talking about. Who is Signor Garibaldi? Not the famed art authenticator, surely."

"The same," Holmes replied, "and part of Sir Johnny's old master swindle. When I was so foolish as to reveal my identity, the man panicked and placed a telephone call—a call which cost four lives, and very nearly a fifth—my own."

All Packwood could do was stare at the detective. Holmes stole a look at Juliet, who appeared lost in thought, before deciding he might safely continue.

"After my visit, Garibaldi's first impulse was to contact Sir Johnny and warn him the cat had escaped the bag, but no one knew where the great man was to be found. For all the authenticator knew, Van Dam had by now learned the wind was up and had already fled the country. His panic doubtless increased. What was the man to do?"

"Then—"

"Ah, but he *did* know his landlord. As I suspected and recently confirmed, Number 12 Cheyne Walk was let to Signor Garibaldi by Glendenning Properties."

"Garibaldi knew Lady Glendenning?"

"More important than that. He knew her coachman—his own accomplice in the old master game, Rupert Milestone."

"But hadn't he learned of Milestone's death from the papers?"

"Signor Garibaldi and his housekeeper were both Italian. You will recall their difficulties speaking English. In all likelihood they didn't take the papers, much less attempt to decipher them. Milestone was Garibaldi's only link to Sir Johnny and, desperate to contact him, he telephoned Lady Glendenning."

"And then . . . ?"

"By this point, trapped in the coils of their treachery, there was no turning back. Like Mr. and Mrs. Macbeth, 'to return were as tedious as go o'er.' Once I confirmed my suspicion who owned Number 12 Cheyne Walk, I understood what happened next. It was Milestone who drove Garibaldi's landlord to 12 Cheyne Walk after dark, where, armed with her own keys Lady Glendenning let herself in via the conservatory door, turned on the gas, and—"

"Oh, God!" Juliet stood up.

"That's enough," I said.

EPILOGUE

"Another scone?"
"I couldn't possibly. Holmes—"
"Coffee?"

"No, really." How was I to broach the subject uppermost in my mind?

"Well, if you should desire another—" Holmes replaced the chafing dish cover and we surveyed one another over the remains of Mrs. Hudson's substantial breakfast, when the detective broke in on my thoughts. "There will always be an aristocracy, Watson."

"What?"

"An elite of blood, or beauty, or brains, or brawn, or a bank balance. It is an inescapable reality."

"You left out talent," I felt bound to point out, which I was pleased to see elicited a blush. "But how did you manage to read my thoughts?"

"Simplicity itself, my dear fellow. I see you continually returning your gaze to stare at poor Rupert Milestone's Rembrandt. The work continues to fascinate and puzzle you. Why was poor Milestone not accorded his due, I imagine you wondering. Hence my attempted answer. There will always be some sort of elite, Watson."

The windows were open and 221B was aired out by a light breeze, cleansed of chemicals and tragedy. Books had been replaced on their shelves and our rooms presently formed an oasis of serenity, as though a tempest had finally cleared. The heart of London on this day seemed as tranquil as Tahiti before the mutiny on the *Bounty*.

Sherlock Holmes sniffed the air with satisfaction. "The first day of summer," he went on, "and all's right with the world. Would you not concur, my dear Watson? And yet I see from your expression that despite my feat of mental legerdemain all is not well with you on this first day of June."

The detective wasn't making my task any easier. "Holmes," I began again, clearing my throat, but he interrupted me once more.

"My dear fellow, I perceive something weighs heavily upon you which you hesitate to lay before me. I assure you, there is no mystery so impenetrable that together we cannot—"

"Holmes, will you kindly allow me to get a word in edgewise?"

He set down his napkin. "Forgive me. What is the matter? Whatever it is, you may depend upon it, I shall do all in my—"

"Holmes!" I now perceived the detective was attempting to forestall what was imminent.

"As you were, old man."

"Holmes," I stuffed my napkin emphatically into its ring, "I have a question to put to you, a matter of vital importance, which will require of you the most careful consideration."

"Heavens, I am all attention, I assure you." Was there a twinkle in his eye?

"Holmes, as you know, I have the honor to be engaged to Miss Packwood—"

"And I have offered my heartiest congratulations. I'm sure you will both be wonderfully happy—"

"Holmes, I am trying to put before you a most important question—"

"And I assure you, my dear Watson, my answer will be *yes*."

"You—yes . . . ?"

"Yes, I will be honored to serve as your best man."

My jaw must have slackened in surprise. "You will?" I had dreaded to pose this request, having not the least idea what my singular friend's response might be, but now I sighed with relief.

"But how did you know?"

"You know my methods, Watson," the detective began, but then threw back his head and laughed uproariously. "I guessed, my dear Watson—I guessed!"

He laughed until tears rolled down his cheeks. I confess the sight unnerved me.

༄

PACKWOOD, JOHN.—on the 24th inst. at St. George's, Hanover Square, by the Rev. Frank Elliot, Vicar of St. Luke's, Osney-Crescent, N.W., JOHN H. WATSON, M.D., Army Medical Department, (Retired), formerly attached to the 5th Northumberland Fusiliers, second son of the late W. E. Watson of Heath Lodge and Dorset to JULIET AGNES PACKWOOD, third daughter of the late COLONEL JOHN PACKWOOD, VC (post.), of the same regiment. After the ceremony, a reception was held for family and friends in Portland Place.

This spare announcement in *The Times* sums up the momentous day but hardly does justice to the emotions that accompanied it. In a semi-transported state, my impressions of the ceremony remain pleasingly hazy, seen as it were, through the wrong end of a telescope. Gerald Packwood gave away the bride, with Holmes, as promised, standing forth solemnly as my best man. Whatever his private feelings on this occasion (those I glimpsed when I first told him of my impending nuptials), he was careful to conceal them and performed his duties admirably, producing the rings on cue. Various former members and messmates of the Fifth Northumberland were in attendance, one or two with pinned armless sleeves and several with walking sticks and eyeglasses by this time. Juliet, looking ravishing in white organdy, carried a bouquet of freesias, later caught by Edith Ayrton,* one of her bridesmaids, after which all retired to a splendid luncheon in Portland Place.

Amid clinking glasses in the merry hubbub, did I spare a thought for that other couple, the doomed landlady and her unfortunate tenant? I don't believe I did. Did the detective? It was at this

---

* Another suffragette, author of the novel *Barbarous Babes*.

moment that I realized my friend was nowhere to be seen. "Where is Holmes?" I abruptly wondered.

"He made his excuses, dearest," Juliet whispered, a hand on my arm.

"He complained of a headache," said Gerald Packwood.

I was disappointed but not surprised. I knew the detective well enough by now to have anticipated such an escape. As long as I had known him, Sherlock Holmes had eschewed both displays of emotion or public acknowledgment. I had often witnessed him shy away before occasions such as this—a diamond stick pin from "a certain gracious lady" at Windsor was his limit. Ceremonies in which he was to participate, or worse, be honored, drove him to seek out anonymity, on one occasion going so far as to decline a knighthood.

Seated amongst the happy company, I realized, with a melancholy jolt, that a momentous change had just taken place. It wasn't only my life that had been upended, it was that of my singular companion's as well. As I contemplated this development and fell to considering the latest alteration in both our lives, Gerald Packwood tapped me on the shoulder. "I believe the champagne is with you, doctor. Will you propose the toast?"

I rose somewhat unsteadily to my feet, struggling to reconcile my newfound joy with the simultaneous loss of something else. During the years I had shared rooms with the detective, it may not have been happiness in any formal definition of the word, but had it not been the next best thing? A comfortable and comforting habit, enlivened at regular intervals by the thrill of the chase?

"Darling . . . ?"

In the press of events I had not thought to plan any words on this occasion and stared with some confusion at the small sea of expectant faces before me. What could I possibly say? Then, as I looked at my glowing bride, the words popped unbidden from my lips. I raised my glass in her direction and said:

"I know the real thing when I see it."

In the applause that followed, I was rewarded with that inimitable smile.

When Earth's last picture is painted and the tubes are twisted and dried,
When the oldest colours have faded, and the youngest critic has died,
We shall rest, and, faith, we shall need it—lie down for an aeon or two,
Till the Master of All Good Workmen shall put us to work anew.

And those that were good shall be happy; they shall sit in a golden chair;
They shall splash at a ten-league canvas with brushes of comets' hair.
They shall find real saints to draw from—Magdalene, Peter, and Paul;
They shall work for an age at a sitting and never be tired at all!

And only The Master shall praise us, and only The Master shall blame;
And no one shall work for money, and no one shall work for fame,
But each for the joy of the working, and each, in his separate star,
Shall draw the Thing as he sees It for the God of Things as They are!
—Rudyard Kipling

ACKNOWLEDGMENTS

Yes, as Holmes lovers will easily note, the cab driver is a nod to Jefferson Hope. The book itself I suppose is a kind of closing the circle on *A Study in Scarlet*, the original Holmes story, which I must have first read when I was about eleven. As I'm thinking this will be my last Holmes novel, it seems fitting to return to the first.

The origins of the present book don't go back quite that far. They can be traced to a turbulent flight from New York to Pittsburgh in 1974, when I was in my twenties. I was on the first leg of a book tour for my surprise bestselling novel, *The Seven-Per-Cent Solution*. In those days, publishers paid for book tours and I landed in Pittsburgh somewhat green from being tossed around, to be met by a local reporter who clearly thought the assignment of traipsing to the airport to interview a kid author was beneath him. As perhaps it was.

ACKNOWLEDGMENTS

Possibly to demonstrate his pique, his first question as we sat down in the airport coffee shop was, "So how does it feel to be a successful forger?"

Nothing could have taken me more by surprise. I recognized the inherent hostility in the question, but as I fumbled to answer, I also got that it made a kind of sense. Now that I thought about it, wasn't I, in fact, a forger, as the reporter's question more than implied? At the time I think I managed to dodge the issue by pointing out that nowhere in the book did I claim authorship of *The Seven-Per-Cent Solution*; rather I labeled myself the "editor." Didn't that, I teased, get me off the hook?

We went on from there somehow. I don't remember what he finally wrote, but as I made it to my hotel and continued my tour, I had to admit the reporter's question—really more an accusation—had got under my skin and stayed there.

I realized that in truth I *was* a kind of forger. Perhaps, as I wrote the novel, I told myself I was playing a game in dreaming up the pedigree and provenance of my "discovered" manuscript, but that couldn't and didn't disguise the fact that I was pretending to have unearthed a missing piece of Watsoniana. Which was, in reality, nothing of the kind.

I *am* a forger.

For the first time, this got me thinking about the whole practice and arena of forgery. Over the years that followed I amassed and read a small library of books on the subject, many of which discussed the questions and tricks practiced in the present volume. As I hope *Sherlock Holmes and the Real Thing* demonstrates, forgery

ACKNOWLEDGMENTS

confronts society with a wealth of confusing technical, legal, aesthetic, and, perhaps most importantly, ethical questions.

Which is why, instead of beginning my Acknowledgements, as usual, by saluting Sherlock Holmes's progenitor, I begin by tipping my hat to that unnamed reporter from Pittsburgh, who first got me interested in the subject of forgery. Writers of Holmes sequels inevitably—and appropriately!—pay homage to Sir Arthur Conan Doyle, the genius who created Holmes and Watson, two of the most beloved characters in all fiction. But given the subject matter of this particular book, I felt I had to lead off with mention of that Pittsburgh reporter. I hope life has treated him well.

Prompted by his provocative question, I have, over the ensuing years, read a great many books about forgers and forgeries. And watched several movies and documentaries on the subject as well. Without intending in any way to honor these rascals, I need to make mention of forgers with names like Van Meegeren, Chatterton, Ossian, Eric Hebborn, Elmyr de Hory, Thomas Keating and Clifford Irving, all of whom may be said to have contributed to this book. There's the outstanding example of Rudy Kurniawan, the Indonesian golf caddy who has the distinction of being the first forger ever sent to prison for forging rare wines. There's *F for Fake*, the wildly entertaining Orson Welles mockumentary, to say nothing of "found footage" like *The Blair Witch Project*. When I lived in London, the British Museum mounted *Fake???* a hilarious exhibition of forged art and artifacts (fish with fur!) that filled several rooms.

Authors like John Brewer, Jonathan Lopez, Fritz Mendax, Alice Beckett, Edward Dolnick, Lord Kilbracken, Frank Arnau, and

ACKNOWLEDGMENTS

others too numerous to mention, have contributed to the literature on this disturbing and perplexing subject.

As a character in the novel muses, there's no telling how many undiscovered fakes adorn the walls of museums and private homes around the world, their authenticity never questioned. And questions posed by those myriad fakers continue to bedevil viewers and collectors—if you can't tell the difference, what *is* the difference?

Possibly only, as someone else remarks in the book, one could not have existed without the other.

And now, thanks to AI, you can more or less forge anything. Even forgers will be put out of work.

Cold comfort.

In addition to fakers and forgers, I must make mention of legendary art dealers, of whom none remains more famous (infamous?) than Sir Joe Duveen, aka Lord Milbank, on whom the character of Johnny Van Dam is partially based. Stories of Duveen's salesmanship abound. The tale of the eight Rembrandts is part of Duveen mythology, supposedly unloaded on none other than Marshall Field, the department store magnate, who came from Chicago to New York to consult with the art dealer and wound up with much more than he dreamed of bargaining for. Duveen's "authenticator" was the equally celebrated Bernard Berenson. The symbiotic relations between the two men are chronicled by Colin Simpson in his surprising account, *Artful Partners—The Startling Story of the Secret Collusion Between the Century's Most Eminent Art Critic and the World's Most Successful Art Dealer.*

I must also acknowledge Catherine Cooke of the Sherlock Holmes Society of London and David Robb, the indispensable

ACKNOWLEDGMENTS

reader of my audiobooks, (in my judgement the perfect Watson).

Special thanks to Lynn O'Leary, my friend and docent at the Getty Museum in Los Angeles. It was Lynn, whom I first met when she was in charge of DVDs at Paramount Pictures, who turned me onto the amazing book *The Sale of the Late King's Goods* by Jerry Brotton, which played such an important role in plotting this story. Brotton's notion that Henry VIII's founding of the Church of England, estranging Protestant England from Catholic Europe, was the first Brexit, continues to intrigue me.

In addition to those experts whose books I consulted or with whom I was in personal contact, there's a host of friends who patiently read (and in some cases reread) the manuscript, making helpful suggestions: Paula Namer, Jonathan Tiemann, Jim Sjveda, Richard Rayner, Michael Phillips, Juliana Maio; also and especially Roxanne Meyer, my able and tireless assistant throughout the creation of this book, and more thanks to Madeline Meyer, another daughter, and her new husband, Dan Colanduno, for careful proofreading as well as catches and editorial suggestions.

I owe thanks in addition to Avi Quijada, my media expert, and to Margot Frankel, designer and monitor of my web page.

And I must not omit to thank my attorney, Richard Thompson, my literary agent, the redoubtable and charming Charlotte Sheedy, and my publisher and Editor (capital E), the one and only Otto Penzler. I have thrived on their encouragement, expertise, and critical acumen.

Finally, I must once more acknowledge Leslie Fram, who makes all things possible.

ACKNOWLEDGMENTS

It remains to be said that whatever errors this book contains should not be ascribed to anyone other than me. There are always typos but I hope I didn't commit too many howlers along the way.

NM